THE TIME-WALKER'S JOURNAL : BOOK 1

SUMMER SNOW

By

Will Hogarth

For Sharon

With thanks to
Nicola Lawrence, David Scott,
Joan Strother & Claire Morgan

Chapter One

A young woman stands at the centre of an almost deserted village square. She sways with the storm, which has suddenly descended, as it starts to rage and tear at her. In her right hand, she is reverently holding a shoulder high, and ornately carved wooden staff. She leans all her weight on this staff for support. Her usual proud and graceful posture is no more, as she looks to the ground, her shoulders dropping. To the casual onlooker she looks weary beyond her years. Her hood has fallen back and as the early winter's blizzard swirls in spirals of anger all around, her long, off blond hair is blowing wild and unkempt in the snow filled wind.

"Why?" asks the young woman.

There is no reply.

She shudders with sudden, intense pain.

"Why?" she asks again. "I loved you."

Again, there was no reply.

1

Will Hogarth

The temperature has drastically plummeted with the onset of this, the first real snowfall of winter. But she is no longer able to feel the icy chill of the worst that the seasonal storm is throwing at her. She is no longer able to feel anything, apart from a creeping, painful, warmth that radiates from a deep savage wound in her upper abdomen, a wound from where a dagger now protrudes. Accompanying this is another pain that burns to her core. The painful realisation of the fact that she had been so totally and utterly betrayed stabs at her heart. It had been a betrayal by someone that she had both loved and trusted. By someone that had been such a pivotal part of her life.

It had not been a frenzied attack or a foolish slash. Instead, it had been a single deadly, upwards thrust that drove the blade home. She had been stabbed by someone who knew what they were doing and had experience with a blade. It had been premeditated murder.

Had her assailant said something to her as they had stepped forward to drive the blade home? Or had it just been their warm, traitorous, breath upon her face? It had only just happened and already she could not recall.

Her spirit had already started its battle to free itself of the body that kept it shackled in this, the world of the living.

"Why?" She tried to ask once more, but her voice was now no more than an inaudible murmur.

Her inner voice still screamed berating her for not being able to read the signs that had lead to this. She should have seen it coming had she not been too preoccupied with the joyous turn her life had so recently taken.

Reluctantly, as her strength was failing, she released her grip on the staff. It fell without a sound to the snow covered ground. Then she herself fell, first only sagging to her knees, her hands now clutched at the leather bound hilt of the dagger, as it protruded from beneath her long black woollen cloak. All her physical feelings were now dulling. Pain of the betrayal visited upon her was all that remained. This was not supposed to happen, for tomorrow was going to be her day. It was to be a day of joy, a day of celebration for her and the whole village. That was gone now, like smoke on a breeze it had vanished in an instant, along with her own future. She gripped the leather covered handle tighter, and with what remained of her strength, she pulled it free. She opened her hand and watched as it dropped; as spun hilt over blade, to the now deep snow covered ground. A splash of crimson blood accompanied it, soiling the virginal white of the freshly fallen snow.

Removing the blade had fully opened the wound and the blood was now pumping unrestricted from within. Unable to stem the flow with her hand the blood now flowed strong and free from between her fingers. It

3

pumped from the deep diamond shaped wound, from what she considered must be the centre of her being.

As she grew weaker, a single icy chill replaced all other feelings. Still this was not because of the worsening weather. Instead, it was the chill, the hard cold ice, which came from her own mortality, as death stalked its prey and drew ever nearer.

The young blond was no longer able to remain upright and slumped heavily to one side into the ever deepening snow. As her vision started to fade, she watched the faint outline of her assailant flee the scene. They scurried away, vanishing into the storm as its curtains folded around them. They did not even look back at what they had done. She had no thoughts of hatred or contempt. Even in death, she was not that sort of person. Her only thoughts were "How could they do this? How could they betray her?" At last, she fell fully backward and was welcomed into the fresh crisp snow. She would never have answers to these questions, she realised, but they would be her final worldly thoughts.

The blood continued to flow. More of a slow ooze now, taking her life force with it, she knew her time was done. She now belonged to eternity and death was inevitable.

Just then, at the dawn of her final moment, a bright light intruded upon her failing vision. Then a booming rush of wind assaulted her ears and finally both these were accompanied by a smell of ozone that filled her nostrils. It was a smell that reminded her of the high mountain storms of her childhood homeland. Her lips, ever so slightly, curved up at the corners as she gave a faint smile and tried to call out. But sound was now beyond her as she choked on her own blood, as it bubbled in her throat and mouth.

Her heartbeat slowed. It stuttered. Then it struggled to its final beat. This was it. This was the end...

Chapter Two

ife was not fair for Steve Thyme. Well that's how he saw things. This glass and broken glass at that, was just another one of those life events that seemed to prove the point.

Steve Thyme looked down at the devastation he had once again caused and stared in utter disbelief. It wasn't fair. Why did this keep happening to him? Why did nothing seem to go right in his life? It was broken glass now, but moments ago it had been a perfectly normal window in the cottage that his parents had rented for the summer. Now it was nothing more than shards of glass. They were scattered over the freshly turned flower border. They surrounded an old and tatty football which had been the offending item in this, his current tragedy.

Steve blinked. Then he closed his eyes, squeezing them tight, as if this could erase what had just happened. As if it would turn back the hands of a clock and with them time itself, but he knew he was being foolish and it would do no such thing. He knew he was about to be in trouble again. He was always in trouble these days. He finally opened his eyes once more and yes, all remained the same.

"Why?" Steve asked aloud, and to know one in particular.

Steve was dressed in faded black jeans and a vintage sex pistols: never mind the bollocks tee shirt. It was his attempt at being a bit of a teenage rebel, a try at shaking his geeky persona. He was tall for a boy of fourteen. He had grown almost six inches in the last school term. This was handy as he had been moved ahead a year at school, leaving him feeling physically out of place. He also sported a thin line of soft, fine hair on his top lip. Even though this was only just visible, he was still proud of it. Although Steve had shot away in height, he had not been able to pack on any muscle. Not in the way that marked the onset of manhood in the majority of his older classmates. He had off blonde hair, which hung lank and was well past needing a haircut. Protruding from beneath his hair was a slightly crooked nose. This had been broken earlier the previous term by Smithy, the school bully. The overall look gave Steve a very gangling, even lanky appearance. Well that was how his mother had started to describe him. "Lanky!"

The problem was that ever since his recent growth

spurt, Steve had struggled to master any real form of coordination. If something could be kicked over, knocked off or dropped then it was inevitable that Steve would kick it over, knock it off or drop it. It was almost as if his hands and feet were not where his brain assumed them to be. If this was what growing up was all about, thought Steve, he would be glad when it was all over with. Then he could just get on with the rest of his life.

Now though, through his awkward clumsiness Steve was once again about to end up in deep trouble. For the second time in as many hours, he was going to have to sit and listen to his mother deliver one of her scolding lectures. It was often said, by his father anyway, that Mrs Jane Thyme, his mother, could scold for her Country.

It just wasn't fair. These things just seemed to happen and it wasn't his fault. After all it had been his mother that had chased him outside in the first place.

"Go and get some fresh air." she had said, "And get out from under my feet."

It was not Steve's fault that outside was not a natural environment for him to find himself. He was as far from an outdoors sort of person as someone could possibly be. He was much more at home with his precious books and a computer than with being outdoors. He took after his father and was a natural academic. He excelled at school. He was a natural at languages, at maths and science and due to his father's career, history, but he most definitely, did not excel at sport or any other activity that needs to take place outdoors.

It had only been forty minutes since his mother had chased him outside. This was after he had ended up in her way one too many times during her cleaning of the house. Her exact words, at the end of a lecture that had seemed to go on forever were "For goodness sake Steven Thyme! Get out from under my feet. Get out that door. Out into the sunshine and find something else to do rather than mope round here."

So outside Steve had found himself, he was still moping around, but outdoors now rather than in, and more so now. With his hands thrust deep into his baggy jeans pockets, he scratched at the dusty ground with one foot. He was bored. In Steve's opinion, it just wasn't fair. It was the summer holidays after all. He was supposed to be on his vacation like every year. They should be on the family's summer tour of Europe, but this year, for the first time in his life, that he could ever remember, it was not to be. It just wasn't fair! Yes, his parents had taken the time to take him to one side. Yes they had explained how their investments had gone wrong and had not performed as well as they had expected. They continued to explain that how, rather than taking summer leave from his post as lecture of History and Archaeology at the University. Steve's father was going to have to go on the department's annual summer dig to earn some extra money. Then his mother had added; how the rest of family would be joining him so they could still have their summer together. As far as Steve was concerned, it still wasn't fair. Plus, Steve thought that his father was secretly looking forward to digging round in the muck; he was that sort of bloke.

So for the summer his parents had rented one of a small collection of cottages that made up the excuse of a village of Ravensby in North Yorkshire. The village was situated less than a couple of miles from the universities dig site. Ravensby was typical of an 'off the beaten track' country village and comprised of a collection of small cottages. Some of them like theirs, painted white and thatched. Others built of a local grey stone with slate roofs. The small village also included a public house, come Inn, and a youth hostel, most often frequented by hill walkers, up on the hill. The village of Ravensby was as far away from real civilization as Steve could imagine being.

Steve's mother had insisted that they had been lucky to get the cottage. Most people helping out at the dig had to make do with sharing dormitories at the youth hostel.

"After all, it was a rather stunning part of the British countryside just off the northeast coast." she had said.

"Yeah, lucky." Steve repeated in a sarcastic tone that had been totally lost on his mother.

Steve had been standing in their cottage's small

walled garden. He was wishing that he was somewhere else, anywhere but where he was. Then after a few minutes, he decided he needed to find something to do. Anything that would relieve the boredom would do. Steve looked round the garden that was positioned to the rear of the cottage. It reminded Steve of tacky chocolate box lids sold in village gift shops. It was small and traditional. It was a painted white and thatched country cottage with a single window positioned to each side of the bright red painted, stable styled, rear door. A black horseshoe was pinned above the door for luck. Above the ground floor and in the thatched roof, there were the two small windows of the upper-floored rear bedroom. It was Steve's room and where he preferred to spend his time given any choice. The garden itself was surrounded on three sides by a chest high wall. This was also clad in a similar crude, white, lime plaster to that of the cottage. Within the confines of the wall, most of the garden was taken up by a large central lawn area. The lawn was starting to turn more yellow than green in the harsh summer sunshine, a summer that the news was already calling a record-breaking heat wave. Surrounding the lawn were a series of well-tended, and freshly dug flowerbeds. Planted in beds, at irregular intervals, were various coloured roses. Steve thought the whole thing looked tacky.

A small decaying wooden shed, approximately six feet

by four feet, stood in one corner of the garden away from the cottage. Its once bright green paint flaking away from the drying and cracked wooden construction.

Since there was nothing else of interest, at least nothing that caught Steve's eye, he had been drawn over to the shed. What harm could it do after all? On initial inspection, the door was bolted, but it was not locked. Although it was an old bolt, it was well oiled and easily slid to one side allowing the door to swing out and open. The first scan of the sheds interior revealed nothing interesting. It seemed to contain nothing but gardening and other tools, like any other shed across the country. The tools were neat, and stacked against the sides or hung on makeshift hooks that had been screwed to the internal strengthening battens and cross members. It was during a second look round and a more thorough rummage that Steve spotted the football. It was wedged behind a fork and spade set in a corner, at the rear of the dark interior. It was old, scuffed and greying with age. It could have been so easy to miss within the dimly lit interior of the shed, and Steve would come to wish that he had missed it. But no, there it was, an old football. Steve had picked it up and returned to the garden.

Steve was not a sporty type, though he was also sick of having nothing to do and of being bored. So he started kicking the ball off one of the garden walls with a steady and slow rhythmic tap, tap, tap. With each sound of the ball rebounding from the wall, Steve had started to think. He stewed things over in his mind. This in turn caused his mood to fester. Tap, it just wasn't fair. Tap, why did he have to be here in the middle of nowhere? Tap, why did his father have to work this summer? Tap, why weren't they on holiday in Europe like they were supposed to be? Tap, it just was not fair. Tap.

With this mood building and the thoughts swirling round in his mind, Steve's anger started to build. Each kick of the ball grew progressively harder. Each tap off the wall grew louder. Steve allowed his thoughts to twist and contort in his mind. Then he had given the ball an almighty kick. Not an opportune moment for the uncoordinated side of Steve to make an appearance, but appear it did. The ball sliced off Steve's right foot. It arced at an almost impossible angle. It headed straight towards the cottage. Not just the cottage, at the window that was to the right of the slightly ajar rear door. After watching the ball fly for what seemed a lifetime, as time seemed to slow and realizing its trajectory, but at the same time hoping against hopes to be wrong, the ball made contact. It struck the window. At first it compressed, just a little against the glass then more, then what followed was a loud, gut wrenching cracking sound. Then the ball fell away in a shower of glass. The window had shattered.

Steve stood there with a feeling of dread. Way down in the pit of his guts, the dread of someone resigned to

13

and awaiting their doom. It was the dread of someone waiting for the consequence of an ever-approaching inevitability. As the moment stretched out so did the feeling. It wrenched and rived. It ate at him. It routed him to the spot neither able to, nor daring to flee. Steve just stood there and waited.

Then the sound he was both waiting for and at the same time dreading. It was the familiar sound of his mother's voice. It was at full volume. It was also several octaves above the norm. It was that so frequent tone of late and one that he had grown to fear. With every syllable of his name stressed to give extra emphasis.

"Steven Thyme. Get in here. Now." called his mother.

Chapter Three

With his hands thrust deep into his jeans pockets Steve hung his head low. He made his way slowly into the cottage and tried to prolong the moment. Steve hoped to put off facing his mother. As if the delay would in some way lessen his mother's wrath. Leaving the garden, he entered through the rear door. This opened straight into a typical country kitchen. Complete with a Belfast sink and large traditional range style cooker. He passed the rustic kitchen table. Then he exited through an internal door into the adjoining dining room. This was a more formal room and Steve had to squeeze past a highly polished, oak, dining table and chairs. A large, ornate, inglenook fireplace in the main wall dominated the dining room itself. Even though there was no need for a fire in the current heat wave, it did look the part thought Steve as he lingered, putting off the inevitable. As Steve approached the door that would allow exit from the dining room, he heard his mother call once more. This time louder and with what seemed more anger than before. "Steven."

The sound of his mother's voice convinced Steve that the best policy may be just to get this over and done with. He needed to face his mother and take the lecture. That would be it and it was becoming obvious to him that any delay was just going to make the matter worse. So with this new resolve, Steve decided to put his best foot forward and get a move on. The thing was that it wasn't his best foot. It was just at that very inopportune moment that Steve caught his foot on a small black cast iron doorstop, in the shape of a Scottie Dog. With his hands still in his pockets, Steve had no way to steady himself. He crashed against the door. Then he hit the wall. Then finally he ended up on the floor. He lay there tangled in the remains of a large pot plant that he managed to knock over on his way down.

Steve did what can be best described as a good impression of an upturned tortoise. He thrashed around a bit at first before managing to get his hands out of his pockets. Then with this minor triumph, he eventually got up from the floor. In the haste to open the door though, Steve failed to get his foot out of the way quick enough. It took three attempts to open it, as it kept rebounding shut, off his foot.

By the time he did manage to get himself, through a

now opened door, into the small hallway that led to the living room, Steve found himself face to face with his mother. She had obviously been alerted by the crashing calamity in the dining room and had come to investigate what was going on.

At first, they stood there, saying nothing, in the hallway. Steve and his mother faced each other. The front door was to one side, which lead out onto the riverside path. To the other side was a narrow steep staircase, leading up to the second floor. Steve stared at his mother. He was breathing deeply and still trying to collect himself after his involvement in the carnage in the living room. In turn Steve's mother stared back, but she was not staring at Steve he soon realized. She was looking over his shoulder and passed him. Steve slowly turned around to look back at what his mother could have been so engrossed in. Then the full extent of the dining room incident hit him. The plant from the upturned pot was shredded beyond recognition; the pot was broken into at least a dozen pieces of brown and cream painted terracotta. The soil from the pot was everywhere. His frantic scramble to his feet had obviously made this much worst. Then looking up Steve also spotted the grubby handprints on the white walls where he had steadied himself on standing. With thoughts of 'oh my God' and 'it just isn't fair' in his mind, Steve turned back and faced his mother. She was now

17

looking him full in the face.

By now his mother's face was almost the colour of the door from which Steve had entered the cottage. Her eyes bulging like two oversized saucers. She turned on her heels with her mouth contorted into a grimace of anger from which she finally spat three words. "Come with me!"

"I'm sorry mum." Steve said.

"Just come with me!" was his mother's only answer.

Now worried to the pit of his stomach again, Steve followed his mother into the living room. This was the largest room in the house. It was comfortably furnished with three large, over stuffed, sofas. A scattering of antique looking oak furniture completed the look. No two pieces matched but as a collective they added to the overall comfortable and homely feel of the room. An ornate fireplace was in the centre of one wall and display cabinets stood in both alcoves filled with curiosities and keepsakes that the owners must have collected over generations. His mother had come to a stop just in front of the window that overlooked the walled garden. The window which was now broken and she sighed. This was not in anger; instead it was a sigh that cried in volumes of disappointment. Steve looked at the window. Then he looked down at a small white figurine. The impact had knocked it off the windowsill and it lay amongst the glass. Then he looked back to his mother and he felt ashamed. This was not a feeling Steve was expecting.

After all it wasn't fair. Steve would have normally insisted that it was not his fault. After all it was his mother that had chased him outside in the first place, all the same, that is how he now felt. He was ashamed.

Steve's mother audibly exhaled. Then she sat down on the arm of the sofa closest to the window and said nothing. Just sat. Although larger than life, Jane Thyme was in fact a small framed woman with a head of fiery red hair. She was a torrent of raw energy and was almost always dressed in an apron. She obsessed over cleanliness, cleaning house and cooking. She ran the house. This was her domain and she was the one in charge. Steve and his father lived in it and around the order his mother created. She had resigned her post at the university, where she had met Steve's father, when Steve had been born. She had never gone back to work after her maternity leave. And she was definitely known for a temper that matched the colour of her hair.

Time dragged on as Steve stood expecting the worst, and then when his mother spoke, Steve was shocked at the soft resigned tone of her voice.

"Get it tidied up." she said, "Just, get it tidied up. Then you can speak to your father about it in the morning."

Then she stood, taking another look around the room. With a sad resigned look on her face, and without saying another word, she turned and left.

Feeling ashamed of what he had done, Steve started to tidy up the mess. With care he picked up the glass that had fallen on the inside of the window and placed it in a small bronzed metal waste bin. He picked up the small white figurine that had somehow managed to remain intact. On closer inspection it was a figure of a young girl and a man that dwarfed her in comparison. It felt unnatural and cold to touch. It was so cold that Steve almost dropped it again. He only avoided doing so by an almost juggle of a catch. Steve quickly placed it back on the windowsill. Then he rubbed his hands together to warm them before straightening out the heavy curtains that hung down to the floor. He made sure that he had picked up all the pieces of glass. Then he made his way back through the house the way he had come. He stopped to pick up the pieces of broken plant pot, the shredded plant and as much of the spilt soil as he could by hand. This too he placed in the waste bin. Looking around for a means to pick up the rest of the soil Steve spotted a small hand brush and dust pan on an ornate brass stand next to the fire place. Steve proceeded to brush up the last of the spilt soil. Then he dusted the dirt off the wall with the end of his tee-shirt. All of the time with the image of his mother's look of disappointment in his head.

When Steve walked through the kitchen and passed his mother, who was standing over the stove, she didn't even look up. Steve walked out into the walled garden feeling worse than ever. He felt lower than if his mother had gone off on one of her rants. Worse than he could remember feeling before. After picking up the last shards of glass from the flower bed Steve returned to the house. Again he passed through the kitchen. Again he passed his mother and again she did not look up or speak to him.

Steve paused, intending to speak but decided against it. It was so and with a very heavy heart that Steve left and climbed the narrow staircase to the first floor landing. He opened the door opposite and entered his bedroom. The room was long and thin. It was almost the full length of the rear of the cottage with two small windows that overlooked the walled garden. It was a sparsely furnished room, with a bed at one side with an adjacent door. There was a desk on the opposite side on which sat Steve's laptop. Two bookshelves and a small wardrobe were arranged against the wall opposite the windows. Apart from the furniture the room was finished with a large, Indian style, rug centrally placed over the well-worn, bare oak floorboards. Steve flopped onto his bed and gave out an audible groan.

It was only early evening but Steve was not in the mood to do anything in particular and being Thursday his father and the rest of the team from the dig site would be in the pub till late. So at least he would not have to speak to his father that night. So Steve just lay on the bed and dozed in and out of a restless sleep, thoughts drifting back and forth between those of shame and the fact that his life just wasn't fair.

Steve woke sometime later, evident by the fact that it was now dark outside. It was the sound of raised, arguing, voices down stairs that had woken him. It was his mother's voice followed by the quieter and more deliberate voice of his father. It sounded like he was trying to calm her. The old thick walls of the cottage muffled the voices somewhat. This meant the conversation was mostly incoherent to Steve's ears, apart from the odd word or phrase.

"Steven, we've had this conversation before..." from his mother, trailing off into an inaudible murmur.

"But Jane." argued his father, "Not me or my father..." then again into inaudibility.

"What about your Grandfather, Tyler?" Countered his mother. It was in this way the partially heard conversation continued for some time. It was only when their voices were raised Steve caught snippets of the conversation, then their voices dropped as quickly as they had been raised and nothing apart from a muffled low toned murmur could be heard. During this Steve just lay there with his eyes closed and pulled a pillow over his head in an attempt to shut out their voices, he knew it was him his parents were arguing about.

Eventually the voices became quiet and then there was the sound of two sets of footsteps climbing the stairs. A distinctive click of his parents' bedroom door opening and closing signalled that they had gone to bed. Moments later the house was silent and in darkness.

Due to the fact that Steve had slept on and off for the past few hours he was not really that tired. So he lay on his bed still dressed in his jeans and tee-shirt and watched the night sky. It was as clear as the day had been sunny. The lack of light pollution in such an out of the way place resulted in a night sky that was totally bejewelled with stars. Steve watched the constellations of the summer sky take shape. First there was Draco the dragon, then Capheus the King and Cassiopeia the Queen and in time, as Steve watched the constellations in the night sky, he thought: yes, no matter how he dressed and rebelled, he was still a geek. With that thought, Thursday passed slowly into Friday and Steve finally drifted off to a troubled sleep.

Steve ran and ran. He was trapped in an unnervingly cold greyness, a greyness that faded to the bone white of the long dead. Walls pressed in from what seemed to be all sides causing a deep pressing feeling of claustrophobia that seemed to crush the air from Steve's lungs. Still Steve ran, sprinted, blindly on.

The translucent greyness continually shifted. It never

settled or took shape, not long enough to be made out. Then it slightly lifted, as if an unfelt breeze was thinning a morning mist. Then he was running through a solid labyrinth of the same bone-white greyness. The path twisted and turned and Steve continued to run. He didn't know why he was running. He just knew his life depended upon it. If he stopped it would be over. So onwards he ran. Steve ran ever faster. His legs and lungs screamed in a unison of pain, but he was unable to stop or even slow down. So, on he ran twisting and turning at each and every corner. First left and then right, and then left once more.

Steve ran ever on. Out of the once again descending and shifting greyness came a guttural, blood curdling, scream. It was a call of animalistic rage. The scream echoed from wall to wall and then back on itself, reverberating endlessly on a wave of sound. So Steve ran. Then once again the scream came, this time closer and then again, closer still.

A rhythmic drumming joined the sounds of the screams. It was a drumming which grew into a deafening tempo. Now at a volume that vibrated through Steve's whole body, the drumming, the sound of Steve's pounding heart. His heart was racing now as it struggled to provide the oxygen that was needed to saturate the blood in order to keep him running. On and on Steve ran and ran; lungs, legs and chest, now all screaming in an ever heightening tempo of pain.

Steve couldn't stop. He did not want to die and he knew his life depended upon his escape. He had to keep running.

Then it happened. The ever present curse of clumsiness once more raised its ugly head. Steve caught his foot on something partially obscured by the continually swirling, shifting. It looked like a small dog, a black dog, a Scottie dog.

Steve started to fall. He tumbled forward in what seemed like a never ending moment. Time stretched out as Steve himself stretched out. The animalistic scream of rage was now upon him, surrounding him, as he continued to fall. The smell of wet animals filled his nostrils and Steve knew he had failed. He knew his life was forfeit. He fell slowly to the ground, his hands reaching out for protection against the inevitable impact. Then he reached the ground crumpling with the pain of the impact. The pain of the run and the realization of failure added to that of the impact. The bleached white greyness of the dead closed in. Now closer and closer it enveloped him. The screams of rage, the animalistic smells and rage, were now there, crashing in upon him.

Sitting bolt upright in his bed Steve let out a gasp of a long held breath. He was still dressed in his now sweat soaked clothes, his heart pounded and the vivid pain of his dream was still fresh in his mind. Steve looked round to get his bearing and make sure all was how it should be. Eventually Steve sighed as he calmed and then finally he relaxed and fell back to his pillows.

Chapter Four

*F*ollowing his dream, Steve had changed into a fresh tee-shirt and shorts and climbed back into bed. Although he had woken from the dream soaked with sweat he now felt cold. Almost like there was a frost in the air, but that was silly it was summer and in the middle of a record-breaking heat wave to be exact. It must have just been the dream Steve thought to himself. It was still playing mind tricks. Steve closed his eyes and dosed back off into a restless night of dream interrupted sleep. None of the dreams were as vivid as the one that had woken him, so he could not recall any of the details from any of the other dreams. The only thing he was sure of was that they still managed to disturb his sleep for the rest of the night.

The next morning, after struggling through a state of semi-consciousness and constant clock watching Steve finally sat up and climbed out of bed. Almost at once he sat back down. His legs were sore. They felt the same as when the school sports teacher had decided to pick on him and make him do more than he was physically capable of. He hadn't done much the previous day, surely playing with the football couldn't have caused this. Steve rubbed his legs and got up again. This time taking the extra time to stretch out.

One of the things Steve liked about his room in the cottage was that it had an en-suite shower room. It wasn't very big and didn't have any windows. It was more of a converted cupboard really, but it was still good to have his own place to get ready in the morning, away from his parents. It was a chance for some level of independence. Steve showered. He took time to relax his sore legs in the warm water before drying and returning to his room to dress. After initial reaching for his normal garb of black jeans and offensive slogan adorned retro punk tee-shirt, Steve gave pause for thought. He was already in trouble. He would have to face both his mother and father. Neither of whom liked the way he dressed and always commented on it. So instead Steve took the safe route of a pair of blue jeans and a plain inoffensive white tee-shirt from his wardrobe, and dressed.

As he moved around his room Steve could here muffled sounds emanating from downstairs. It was the sounds of his parents talking and the sounds of breakfast being prepared. Steve procrastinated about going down stairs looking for things that needed doing in his room. He even made his bed and tidied yesterday's clothes into a laundry basket, something that he never did. But there was only so long he could put off going down to face his parents and that moment was announced by his mother's call. "Steven, breakfast!"

Steve descended the stairs and made his way through the dining room. He paused for a moment and took a deep breath. Then finally, he entered the kitchen where the family took their breakfast together. As he entered Steve spotted his mother with her back to him. She was stood at the stove, frying something that smelt like a combination of bacon and sausage. The aroma filled the room and caused Steve's belly to pronounce his hunger with a loud rumble. It reminded him that he had gone up to bed the previous night without having anything to eat.

Steve made his way to a small wooden table where his father was already seated, reading the morning paper. Being on the dig; mornings were not the same as in term time. His father did not go into work before Steve got out of bed. Instead he took breakfast with Steve and his mother. He then headed up to, what Steve had gathered to be, a Viking dig site at about ten in the morning. Steve pulled out the chair opposite his father and sat down. His father did not even look up. Maybe, thought Steve, his father, his parents, were not going to say anything. Maybe he had managed to get away with the chain of events that had unfolded the previous day. Maybe his luck was in for a change. With his mood slightly lifting Steve pulled himself closer to the table and looked forward to one of his mother's full English breakfasts.

By now Steve's mother had plated up and was carrying two breakfasts across the kitchen. Steve's father closed and neatly folded his paper setting it down, next to his place setting. The breakfasts were set out before them and Steve's mother returned to the stove to clean it down. She had, as normal, had her more healthy breakfast of cereal and juice long before Steve or his father had come down stairs. The breakfast comprised of bacon, smoked but not salty, cooked crisp but not burned, two fat full flavoured pork sausages, bulging in the skins and still slightly sizzling, and a light poached free range egg on a round of wholemeal toast. This was all complimented with mushrooms and artistically cut and grilled tomatoes on the side. All in all a breakfast of kings thought Steve. As Steve hungrily tucked in he noticed how quiet it was in the kitchen. How quiet his mother and father were. There were none of the normal morning pleasantries. Or any of the banter that normally took place between his mother and father when they breakfasted together. There was just a silence that was becoming more uncomfortable as it continued.

As Steve made quick work of his breakfast, his mother once again approached with two glasses of freshly squeezed orange juice and set them down on the table. She again left without saying a word. Steve swallowed the mouth full he was chewing and washed it back with a big gulp of the juice. Still neither of his parents spoke. So it was in silence that Steve finished his breakfast and juice. Then in turn he watched his father slowly and methodically finish his own. He focused first on the bacon. Then he ate the egg. Then in turn each element on his plate until he too had finally cleared his plate.

Steve broke the silence, "Dad....", but he was cut off by his father's raised hand.

"Come with me." said Steve's father. He then stood up from the table and started to head towards the door that led out into the walled garden. Steve quickly stood. He scraped his chair on the stone floor of the kitchen and came close to knocking it over in the process. He managed to catch it at the last moment and quickly headed out the door following his father. The feeling of dread now returned to the pit of his stomach.

Steve's father, his namesake, was a tall, slim man. He was also thoughtful and methodical, unlike Steve. He was the sort of person who seemed to have a plan for most eventualities. Both the students he taught and his co-workers at the university, where he worked, had nothing but respect for him. He had met Steve's mother, the then Jane Taylor, nineteen years earlier. He had been twenty nine and his mother had been just nineteen. Although there had been ten years between them; they had been together ever since.

Following from behind, in the bright morning sun, Steve watched the purposeful way in which his father walked. It was as if every step was given exacting thought on where it should be placed. Each step was uniform and precise. He was like this in every aspect of his life. Which explained why, his mother and father hit it off so well. Jane who strived for cleanliness and Steve Senior who provided the order. Steve on the other hand was a polar opposite to both his parents. He was messy and all legs and arms, which tripped him up at every opportunity. Steve's parents had been trying for a child for some time when Steve had come along. It had been a difficult birth. This explained why Steve was an only child and to some degree why his mother, Jane, had not gone back to work.

Steve had not really been paying attention in the direction they were heading. Instead he had been watching his father's back to try and gleam some clue to what he was thinking, to what may be about to come. So it was with a start that Steve had to stop when he reached the shed in the corner of the garden. Steve's father opened the door and reached inside to a wooden shelf just to the left of the door. He retrieved a small hammer and a box of tacks. These, without a word, he passed to Steve. Steve took them without a word in return. Next his father went to the side of the shed. It was the side which was close to the garden wall. He reached in and produced a small sheet of plywood. Then after closing up the shed, he silently turned on his heel and headed past Steve back towards the house.

When they came to a stop for a second time they were in front of the broken window. Steve's father turned and spoke. "Steven." He said. "You really need to start growing up. You need to take responsibility for your actions."

"But, dad..." Steve responded, just to be cut off by his father.

"No. Let me finish." Continued his father, "You are getting into trouble far too often you're having more clumsy accidents than anyone I know. Plus you're upsetting your mother far too many times. You know what she's like."

"Yes." Steve responded, now looking down at his own feet.

"Well, it has to stop!" Said Steve's father. "There." Handing Steve the piece of plywood that he brought from the shed. "You can start by boarding up this window. And be careful; I don't want you upsetting your mother again today."

So this was it thought Steve. This was his punishment, fixing, well boarding up the window he had broken. This wasn't too bad. It could have been a lot worse. Steve took care and placed the board over the broken pane of glass. It was almost a perfect fit. This did not surprise Steve, knowing the thoughtful and methodical approach his father had to all aspects of life. Steve held the spare tacks in his mouth, as he had seen his father do on previous occasions. Then held the plywood board in place with the heal of his hand while holding a tack in place. He made sure it would miss the glass but pierce the wooden frame. Steve took one more look at his father who nodded and Steve drove the tack home. He then managed to repeat this process a number of times without incident, securing the board in place.

Steve was not the best person for this type of work. A combination of clumsiness and lack of experience left him feeling ill at ease with the whole thing. It had taken him over half an hour, to do what would have taken his father, maybe, ten minutes. Now he was sweating. This was partially due to the pressure of been so closely watched by his father and therefore not wanting to mess things up. This combined with carrying out manual labour, in the morning sun which, even at this early hour, was already hot. Overall an uncomfortable experience but it could have been worse though, thought

Steve, a lot worse.

Thinking his punishment, and his talking to from his father were complete, Steve turned and started to walk away. He headed back towards the backdoor, then the sudden sound of his father's voice suddenly pulled him up.

"Steve!" called his father, "We haven't finished."

Steve turned back to face his father, wondering what more his father could want. How else was he to make amends? "Yes dad."

"Your mother and I have been talking." started Steve's father, "And we both believe you need to be doing something this summer. Rather than just moping around the house. I don't want you getting in your mothers way."

"But dad…" Interjected Steve

"No, here me out." continued his father, "It's going to be a long summer and there's not a lot to do round here. Even I appreciate that."

"Yes?" answered Steve.

"We both believe that the best use of your time would be to help me at the dig. There are other volunteers helping. You may even end up enjoying it."

"The Viking dig?" Asked Steve, almost blurting it out.

"Yes." said Steve's father, "Unless you're aware of any other digs going on around here."

Will Hogarth

"It's not fair. It's the holidays." Steve tried to insist.

"That it may be." Countered Steve's father. "But at the dig you'll be. You have ten minutes to get ready. Your mum has prepared your lunch."

Steve was dumfounded. That was it. No reasoning or arguing. He was going to be spending the summer helping out at a boring archaeological dig of a suspected Viking settlement. Great, not!

Chapter Five

The archaeological dig site Steve's father was working on was only a short distance from the village. It was about two miles at the most and Steve's father insisted in walking it each day. He stated "The exercise was good for you." So it was that Steve and his father exited the small walled garden and onto a narrow lane. Although it was, in fact, not much more than a dirt track, that ran along the rear of their cottage and a number of others in the row.

Steve's father walked in his normal, deliberate and thoughtful manner. Each step he took was placed as if it had been mathematically planned in advance. Steve walked at his side with his hands, as usual, thrust deep into his jeans pockets. All the time he tried his best not to stumble on the uneven surface.

More than once Steve tried to speak to his father as they walked. He wanted to object to what he considered to be his unjust punishment, "Dad ..."

But he was just to be cut off with a raised hand and a shake of the head.

"But..."

To be cut off again with a stern glare from his, seemingly brooding, father. So it was, in almost silence, that Steve and his father walked. They took a route along the lane then out at the end, onto a small country road. Then they turned towards the dig-site and the Coast. It was still early, but the sun was hot and starting to move into the uncomfortable heat that would build as the day progressed. The thought of manual work on a day like this did not appeal to Steve at all, but he walked with his father, resolved to a fate that he considered most unfair.

They had been walking in silence for maybe ten minutes or so when Steve's father suddenly started to talk. To fill Steve in on the background of the dig site. Steve's father had talked at great length about the dig before. Initially in the days before they had left for Ravensby. This continued as an almost childlike excitement. Then again, regularly around the dining table during the evening meal or at breakfast. Steve had not bothered listening during those times. Mainly due to the fact that even though his father was just the latest in a tradition of family historians and archaeologists, Steve was plain and simply not interested. He had no intention in following in his father's footsteps into what was considered to be the family trade.

"Steven." Started Steve's father, "You know we are staying in Ravensby?"

"Yes, what of it?" Steve replied.

"Well." Continued his father. "We believe that Ravensby is the site of an early Viking settlement. Also we think that Ravensby Tops, the site of our dig was once an important ceremonial site. We think it dates way back to before the Vikings finally converted to Christianity, in the early eleventh century."

Steve looked at his father with what was supposed to be his best expression of, 'I don't really care'. But his father must have mistaken it for a quizzical look because he continued with his tale. Now in an ever more excited tone.

"We believe that the Vikings landed sometime in the latter half of the ninth century at Raveness. Then not long after moved inland to Ravensby. This would be due to the excellent quality of the land. And of course, its elevated defendable position."

Steve nodded and continued to listen as they walked. His father went on to further flesh out his theories. He explained that place names ending in –by, such as Whitby, Maltby and they believed Ravensby, were normally locations where the Vikings had first settled. There were well over two hundred such place names in Yorkshire alone. He then expanded this to how places ending in –ness quite often signified coastal headlands where the Vikings had landed and also settled.

"But why," enquired Steve when his father had finally paused, "is the dig on Ravensby Tops? It's away from the supposed settlement and not in Ravensby or Raveness?"

"We believe," Said Steve's father, "that the hill was not originally called Ravensby Tops. Well not by the Vikings anyway. We think that the name has evolved over time and that it was originally Ravensby Toppen. Toppen is an old Danish word for Hill."

Steve's father paused for a moment before continuing in an even more excited tone. "We, well I, believe that the Ravensby name itself is an evolution of its original name. I suspect that the original name was Odinsby. This in time gained the R to become Rodinsby, and then eventual evolved into the Ravensby we have today."

"So." said Steve, "The dig you are working on is about proving this?"

"Yes, and more." said Steve's father, "If I am right, that would make Ravensby Tops, Odin's Hill. Therefore it would most likely have had major religious meaning to the Vikings that settled in this area."

"Odin?" said Steve, "As in the God of war and death?"

"Yes," Replied his father, "along with being the god of poetry and wisdom. And being the God that Wednesday, or Wodan's day, is named after"

Steve was just about to ask another question when his father, out of the blue, announced that they had arrived at Ravensby Tops. They stopped for a moment at a heavy metal swing gate that led to a narrow path beyond and then on up the hill, Steve's eyes followed along the way of the path and he got his first look at the hill that was Ravensby Tops. It loomed out of the ground in front of them like a huge slab of rock that had been rammed into the earth by the hand of a giant. Not just that, it also looked as if it had been eroded by a multi-millennium of battering by the elements. Only then had its sides relented and it became sloped in a way that had made it accessible to man. Steve's eyes followed the winding path up the side of the hill until once again the rocks surface was shrouded in a green cloak of grass. Shrubs and undergrowth appeared like decorations on a cake. Then he looked further up again, to the top where stood an ancient copse of beach trees. Beach trees that were currently being circled by a flock of birds that appeared black and silhouetted against the blueness of the sky.

"Impressive." Steve commented.

"Yes." Replied his father, "Very!"

They made their way through the gate, one at a time due to the gate being of a design used to keep live stock from passing. They let it swing closed with a loud metallic clank and started to climb the narrow path up the hill. As they walked Steve noted an uneasy, cool stillness in the air. It had an unnerving effect on him. He stood still for a moment pondering the lack of reason for this but eventually just put this down to the fact they were in the shadow of the rock. The chill was most likely a result of being out of the sun. A loud cry from one of the birds, high above, which he now assumed to be ravens, gave him a start and he quickly caught up to his father. After a short way the path grew steep and gravelly under foot. Steve felt his heart start to pound and his lungs work harder to get the air.

"You need to get out more and get more exercise." Said Steve's father, laughing at Steve's lack of fitness.

They continued on up the steep gravelly path for maybe ten more minutes before they crested the top. Here it started to level out. Its surface was becoming more dirt than gravel.

The path had been winding its way around the hill and Steve was wondering how much further they had to go to get to the dig site when he heard voices ahead of them.

They rounded the next bend and walked into a small makeshift camp. Steve realised that they must have been on the other side of the copse of trees that he had noted from the bottom of the hill. The camp was small and comprised of a number of large, old fashioned canvas tents. The one immediately in front seemed to be a communal area for eating, with wooden benches and tables lined up in its interior. To the left of this, separated by a large grey rock that was savagely jutting out of the ground, was a slightly longer tent with a long wooden table inside. It had what looked like items from the dig laid out on it. Further back behind the two main tents and on its own stood a small square tent which Steve assumed to be the digs toilet facility. The thought of which made Steve think he'd prefer to go behind one of the trees rather than share with all the rest of the people on the dig. Especially in the hot weather like they had been having.

Across the top of the hill in the open space a number of areas where digging was already in progress were marked out with white tape. Red flags were positioned in other locations and most people were already busying themselves. There seemed to be a mix of other professionals, like his father. Plus student volunteers amongst the archaeologists. 'Why would people volunteer?' Steve thought to himself. After all he was only here under protest.

At the edge of the dig furthest away from Steve, almost in the copse of trees, a middle aged woman was slowly walking back and forth next to one of the red marker flags. She carried what looked like and industrial scaled metal detector fitted with a screen. Steve looked at his father and was about to ask about what she was doing, but his father who noted the interest said "Come with me and I'll introduce you to Professor Anderson.

They crossed the dig towards the professor. She

spotted them approaching and stopped what she was doing and waved.

"Hi Steve." Said the professor to Steve's father. "Who's this? Another volunteer?"

"Hi Mary," Said Steve's father, "No, this is my son, Steven he's here to lend a hand for the next few weeks. Jane wants him kept out of trouble."

Steve Groaned at the thought of spending weeks at a boring dig site and having to work through his summer.

"This is Professor Anderson." introduced Steve's father, "She is the teams' resident geophysicist. If you ask nice, I'm sure she'll explain all about it." Steve's father then turned and left leaving Steve alone with the professor.

"Firstly it's Mary." Said the professor in a manner that suggested that she liked to talk and was more than glad to have someone to talk to. Or more likely talk at.

Professor Mary Anderson then launched into a long winded and rather technical, thought Steve, description of what geophysics was. Of how it helped on archaeological sites and saved time by identifying the best locations to dig. How geophysics was the physics of the Earth and its environment. And that she was an Archaeological Geophysicist as opposed to his father who was an Archaeological historian. Then she moved on to describe how she utilized various pieces of equipment for delineation of various phenomena including; buried walls and ditches, burial mounds or graves, along with other disturbances hidden from the human eye. Then she went on in detail, repeating herself. It was her job; using geophysics is to identify likely areas for detailed investigation. These would be marked as follow up areas for conventional archaeological digs, hence the red flags. All through the professors little lecture Steve thought to himself, 'yes I already know this, I've been forced to sit through Time Team on television often enough.' But he let her continue, as let's face it he thought, listening to the professor was always going to be better than any type of manual work.

Just as the professor finished her lecture on geophysics a bell was rang next to the communal tent and the professor added "Time for tea."

Chapter Six

Steve sat in the sun next to the communal tent. He was watching the ravens, which periodically circled high above as if something unseen had disturbed them from their roosts within the copse of trees. His father was sitting inside the tent with the other members of the team. He was talking excitedly to the professor about the area that she had just been surveying. Steve, who was not really interested, just sat back enjoying a quiet moment alone, in the sun, and watching the silhouettes of the birds above.

"Steven!" Called Steve's father from within the tent. "Come here. Quickly."

Steve jumped with a sudden start at the unexpected call from his father that had dragged him out of his trance. He got to his feet and walked into the cooler shade of the communal tent, were his father was still sitting with the professor. Steve was temporarily blinded by the comparative darkness of the interior of the tent, after sitting in the bright sun outside. He had to pause for a moment until his eyes adjusted. Fearing that he would look stupid if he walked into someone or something.

"Sit down here Steven." Said his father indicating the seat next to himself and the professor.

"Dad? Professor?" said Steve as he sat.

"Mary, please." Countered the professor once more.

On the table in front of Steve was a print out of, what Steve assumed to be, the area the professor had just surveyed. 'Watching Sunday teatime television had paid.' thought Steve from the sarcastic corner of his mind. It was a simple greyscale print out of what looked like, to Steve, wavy lines and smudges. Beyond that he could not see much more.

"This is a representation of the area Mary has just surveyed." Steve's father said. "Do you see this slight anomaly? Just here." He indicated, pointing to an area on the far side of the print out.

"Yes." replied Steve after a moment of study. The direction of the lines seemed to deviate slightly at just the point his father had pointed to. It was as if they had been forced to go around something unseen, something that interrupted their flow.

"Well." Said his father. "This is somewhat away from the rest of the discoveries. So it is unlikely that it is anything to do with the main focus of the dig. In fact it may not be Viking at all, though it's worth having a look at. So I would like you to dig an exploratory trench across the area."

"Me?" Said Steve "Why me?"

"As I Said." replied his father, "This may have nothing to do with the main focus of the dig as it's away from the other finds. So I can't spare any of the main team. So you it is."

Steve slumped in his seat. Once again he felt defeated and resigned to his fate.

As Steve's father stood up to leave he passed a small spade to Steve. Unlike a standard garden spade it had a much narrower blade, designed to remove small amounts of dirt at a time. The aim was to risk the least amount of damage to any possible discoveries. Steve groaned again. This was going to be a hard and slow progress.

The professor stood to leave. She gave Steve a look that was obvious meant to imply that he should get up and follow. So Steve pushed himself away from the table, stood and quickly caught up the professor, who was already half way across the site to the area she had been surveying. When they reached the red marker flag Steve stopped expecting the professor to do the same, except she didn't. Instead she continued on toward the copse of trees and stopped only just before the tree line. When she did come to a stop she turned and realised that Steve had not followed her and beckoned him closer. She noted the look of confusion on Steve's face and explained.

"The red flag only marks one corner of the survey site. The area we are interested in is at this side of the site. Closer to the trees."

Steve just nodded and grunted a quick "OK."

"Before you start I'll have to get you a fresh ground sheet." Said the professor. Then she jogged off, towards the second large tent. She returned almost immediately with a large thick folded plastic sheet under her arm.

"What's that for?" Asked Steve, nodding towards the plastic sheet.

"We have to return the site to how it was before we arrived." said the professor, "It's the only way they would grant us a permit to excavate here. You have to carefully cut and remove the turf so it can be replaced when we have finished. Then when you dig out the earth you have to put it onto this sheet so again it is easy to replace. Also, if it turns out to be an interesting trench it makes it easy for someone to sieve the soil, to check for smaller artefacts. Or even any fragments of what may have once been here."

The professor then consulted the print out that they had been studying back at the tent. She removed a small spray can from her pocket and marked out a wide rectangular area on the grass. It was approximately two metres long by one and a half metres wide. "Spray chalk."

she said, "This is where I want you to dig your exploratory trench. It seems to have the best chance of finding something without digging out the whole area."

Steve looked at the area the professor had just marked out. His heart sank into his boots. "All that?"

"Shouldn't be too bad." Replied the professor. "Looking at the survey you will probably only have to go down half a metre or so."

"It's just not fair!" Muttered Steve. His words were lost on the air though, as the professor was already leaving. She was either out of ear shot, or at least she was pretending to be.

Steve, once again resolved to his fate, got started. Not wanting to over exert himself, he started slowly. By using the edge of the spade, he cut the turf into a grid within the confines of the chalk boundary. Then carefully he removed each section and stacked them at the side of the plastic sheet, furthest away from the new trench. As Steve started to dig into the soil that lay beneath the turf he noticed an unusual chill in the air. He even though he caught a glimpse of his breath on the air like it was a frosty morning, but when he looked up to the ravens that were now circling directly above him, the sun was still high and bright in the clear blue summer sky. There was not a breath of wind to chill the day. After looking around for an explanation, Steve put the chill down to the fact he was working so close to the copse of trees. Therefore he must, in some way, be in the shade of the ancient trees and the sight of his breath down to nothing more than his imagination.

Digging the trench was slow going as the earth beneath the turf was hard packed. It resisted the spade as if the ground itself was trying to resist Steve's trespass. After trying to make shorter work of the dig by jumping on the shoulders of the spade only to find that the earth would not give, Steve decided that the best approach would be to remove the earth a thin layer at a time across the whole area of the trench. This would take longer but would not be as heavy work. Steve was in no hurry. If he finished this his father and the professor, or one of the others, would just find something else for him to do.

The chill that Steve had original felt when he had started had now passed. He now very much felt the heat of the summer sun. The sweat from his effort dripped from his nose and brow. It ran down his back like a river leaving his tee-shirt uncomfortably damp. Steve was not at all used to any form of manual work. His father had been right, he was not very fit. Periodically during the day the professor strolled over, as if to check on Steve's progress, but said nothing, before leaving and returning from the direction she had came.

The lunchtime bell sounded at the communal tent and still Steve had not dug down to half the depth the professor had indicated. He had found nothing with any more interest than shiny pebbles and long deserted snail shells. He stiffly straightened up and followed the others to the tent and his lunch. Neither his father nor the professor came to talk to him while he ate. Since he was weary from the digging and knew no one else; he was happy to sit in silence and eat alone. The packed lunch his mother had provided him was devoured in a very short time. Manual work increased the appetite. So when it was gone, Steve lay back in the sun and closed his eyes.

The ringing of the bell that marked the end to the official lunch period woke Steve with a start. He sat up with a feeling he had been dreaming, but could not quite remember what it had been about. Then he thought that if it had been anything like the previous night's dream, maybe it was better he didn't remember. One thing he did note though, was that he once again was feeling a chill. Although this was probably down to the sweat from that mornings work evaporating in the sun.

Not being used to the exertion of exercise never mind the harsh exertion of manual labour, Steve rose slowly and stiffly stretched. He was already dreading what he would be like the next morning. At the same time he did not want to let the others know that he was struggling. He definitely did not want to give his mother and father that satisfaction.

The professor arrived at Steve's trench at just the same moment as Steve. She cast a critical eye over Steve's effort and then asked "Are you OK?"

"Oh, yes!" Steve replied. He tried to sound more upbeat than he felt. Then he picked up his spade he started work again, slowly scraping and digging and hacking at the hard packed soil. All the time he thought to himself, 'It just wasn't fair'.

For two or three more hours, Steve wasn't quite sure how much time had passed; he continued to dig and found nothing. He scraped at the soil, adding it to the growing mound on the plastic groundsheet. Then all of a sudden on scraping away a section of earth, at the top end of the trench closest to the trees, Steve uncovered a small ivory white coloured patch. At first Steve wasn't sure what he was looking at, but after a moment he convinced himself that he had, indeed uncovered something interesting. So he scraped at the area again and the ivory white patch grew into a larger ivory disk. Steve then thought the better of continuing to use the spade. If he was his typical self and managed to break whatever he was uncovering he would not hear the end of it from his father.

Dropping to his knees Steve started scraping and dusting away the dirt with his fingers. He slowly uncovered more of the disk that started to appear to be domelike in shape. Then his thumb penetrated deeper

Will Hogarth

into the soil. Steve thought he had found the end of whatever he was uncovering. So he redoubled his effort scraping and dusting until a ridge appeared. It circled what Steve had originally thought to be the edge then after a couple more minutes of scraping, it dawned on Steve what it was. He had found a skull.

"Dad! Professor!" Steve shouted as he jumped up and stepped back from his find.

Chapter Seven

"**D**ad!" shouted Steve for a second time, before he looked up. He saw his father and the professor running in his direction. Most of the others on the site followed behind. Steve's father was the first to arrive and took care stepping down into the trench, while at the same time he moved Steve out of the way. The professor arrived promptly on his heels, but she just stood at the side peering in. Then all of a sudden the trench was surrounded by almost everyone who was working on the site. Excited muttering could be heard from around the trench. Steve heard all sorts of questions raised from the assembled throng. Academics and students alike pushing in closer on the trench.

"What is it?" Came the question from one observer.

"Is it a body?" Asked another.

"It's a skull." Stated one voice closer to the trench.

"Is it a grave?" Asked someone from the back.

It was the professor that spoke, with a clear

authoritative voice that silenced the others. "Steven has, indeed, found a skull." She said, "But that is all we can see at the moment. We are going to have to excavate further before we can say any more beyond that."

There was a murmur from the crowd. Then the professor spoke again before any further questions could be voiced. "Come on, all of you. Back to your own work. We'll let you know when we find out anything more."

The assembled crowd reluctantly dispersed from the side of the trench. They all started to return to wherever on the site they had been before Steve had called out. Eventually they left just Steve, his father and the professor behind with Steve's discovery.

Steve's father was now on his knees in the trench and, like Steve had been. He was gentle, working at the dirt around the skull with his fingers slowly uncovering more of the ivory coloured bone.

"Steve?" asked the professor of Steve's father.

"Steve?" she asked again when no reply was forthcoming.

Steve's father slowly stood as if it was hard to take his eyes off the skull that was starting to take shape in the bottom of the trench. Then finally he faced the professor.

"We will need to expand the exploratory trench, so we can get a good look and see." Said Steve's father.

"Do you want me to mark up?" asked the professor.

"No." said Steve's father, "I'll take charge here myself."

"What about your son?"

They both turned to face Steve. He was now sitting on the grass, feeling forgotten and left out, behind the trench. On hearing his voice Steve looked up again.

"You've done a good job here." said his father, "This is a good find. Do you want to help me dig it out further?"

The thought of digging out, what may be a full skeleton appealed to Steve, so he answered with a quick "Yeah, you bet."

"We may be here late." he said, "I'd like to get it out the ground before we go home."

"I don't mind." Steve replied.

"I'll text your mother and let her know. We don't want her to worry." Said his father, taking his mobile from his pocket.

"Is it Viking? Is it a grave?" asked Steve in quick succession.

"Too early to tell yet." Came the voice of the professor, "We need to clear more earth before we have any clear ideas in that direction."

The professor turned and walked away in the direction of the tents, while Steve stood waiting for his father to finish texting. His father wasn't very good with technology and Steve was more than a little bit surprised that his father had learned to text at all. It was probably down to his head always being stuck in the past thought Steve.

By the time Steve's father had finished texting, the professor had returned with a loaded up wheelbarrow. She proceeded to unload its contents at the side of the trench. The items included an extra spade, the same as the one Steve had been using, a couple of small trowels, and an assortment of brushes, which ranged from a small nail brush to what almost looked like a broom with a very short handle. Then finally she placed a selection of plastic trays at one end of the trench. Wheelbarrow now unloaded the professor took hold of its handles and wheeled it off again without a word.

Noting Steve's quizzical look his father explained.

"The spades are to do the heavy surface dig." His father said, "But now we know there is something of interest here, so when we start getting close to this level." he indicated to where the skull was uncovered, "We need to be more careful. So that is what the trowels and brushes are for."

"What about the trays?" Steve asked pointing to the plastic trays the professor had just laid out at the end of the trench.

"They are for anything of interest we find. If you're not sure put it in a tray."

Steve nodded.

"We'll start by expanding the trench." said his father,

"To an area that I think will get us what we're after."

Steve's father picked up a spade and Steve followed his lead. His father moved to a position about two metres from the existing trench and dug in his spade. He indicated to a position opposite for Steve to do likewise.

"We'll expand the trench to here." He stated

Looking at the area that they were now going to be excavating Steve gave a small inwards groan. It was going to take his original trench and expand it to two-to-three times the size. This will take ages thought Steve, and they started to dig. Firstly carefully removing and stacking the turf and then into digging out the hard compacted earth that lay beneath.

To his pleasant surprise, Steve's father was stronger than he looked. They were making good progress on what his father had described as 'the heavy dig'. The mound of soil on the plastic groundsheet grew steadily. When the expansion trench they had been digging finally joined up with Steve's original excavation and was almost to the depth of the original, Steve's father raised his hand and signalled a halt.

"You ok?" asked Steve's father.

"Yeah, spot on." Steve replied, and when he thought about it, he was. He was enjoying working with his father. He was enjoying the excavation and the anticipation of what they may find.

So they just sat on the edge of the trench, father and

son, catching the breaths. When Steve looked around he noted that there didn't seem to be as many people around. One or two remained over by the tent, another pinning a plastic protective cover over a trench that they had been working on and then there was the faint shape of the professor sitting at a table in one of the tents. Steve checked his watch and it was now well after five. They had been digging a lot longer than he thought and most of the crew, academics and students, had left for the evening. But it was summer and the sun was still bright in the late afternoon sky.

"Now the fiddly job." said Steve's father picking up a trowel and brush. He indicated that Steve should do likewise.

"What do we do with these?" asked Steve, picking up a trowel and brush of his own.

"We'll start at the skull, that's already visible. You work down the left side while I'm on the right. We'll work down the trench uncovering as we go."

Steve sprang up to start.

"Carefully!" added his father.

They knelt side by side in the trench, progress was slow going, but at the same time it filled Steve with a feeling of anticipation. An expectancy grew as they worked, taking care as they scrapped with the trowels then brushing away the loosened dirt. They repeated over and over again as they uncovered more of the long buried skeleton.

Suddenly Steve's father sat up. Holding something in his hand, he gently brushed at it with one of the smaller brushes. Steve watched in fascination as the soil fell away and slowly revealed what must have been, at one time, an item of immense beauty. The more his father worked at it the more it started to look like a piece of golden jewellery, like a broach or ornate button.

"What is it?" Steve finally asked in a gasp, after seemingly holding his breath while his father worked.

"I think it's a pin." replied is father, still studying the find closely. "The sort of thing that would have been worn, by someone well to do, to keep a cloak fastened."

"Is it Viking?"

"It looks like it could be. Ninth century at that."

He showed the pin to Steve. It was in the form of a man holding a sword in one hand and two spears in the other. The figure was also wearing a horned helmet and on turning it over Steve's father pointed out where the pin fastening would have originally been.

"It probably represents a priest of the cult of Odin." Stated his father, before laying the object carefully in one of the plastic trays.

"You said that you thought this hill had originally been Odin's hill, didn't you?"

"Yes." replied his father, "Let's get the rest of this uncovered, before it gets too late."

They returned to the excavating of the now, almost, uncovered skeleton. Steve was hopeful that he would make a discovery that matched that of his father. Though this was not to be, as by the time the complete skeleton was uncovered, no more discoveries had been made. They both stood and looked at what now lay in the trench.

"It is, or it was, a young woman." Announced Steve's father.

"How can you tell?"

"A woman's pelvis is flatter, more rounded and larger to allow for child birth." Stated his father, "And the rib cage is narrower than that of a man. Plus this is a small skeleton. Which would suggest it is that of a child or a young woman."

"But why a young woman and not an old one?" countered Steve.

"The teeth are in good condition. Plus at a quick glance the joints had not started to deteriorate by the time of death."

Steve nodded, impressed with what his father knew. They were standing looking at the burial of a young ninth century Viking woman.

"There's one thing though." said his father.

"What?"

"I wouldn't have expected a woman to be buried here. Not like this, it's more of a male burial. But that's definitely the skeleton of a young woman."

"But why?" Steve tried to ask.

"Just wait here." said his father, "I need to go and get Mary."

Then added, "And don't touch anything." as an afterthought.

Watching his father heading off towards the tents muttering to himself, Steve stood in the trench. He was at what must, he figured, be the foot of the grave looking at the skeleton. As he stood he felt a chill pass over him. It was late now and the sun was low in the sky and now the exertion of the dig was over, Steve was feeling cold.

Steve picked up one of the small paint brushes and started brushing away small amounts of dirt from around the now fully excavated skeleton. More out of wanting to be doing something than for any other reason. He had only been working for a moment when something metallic caught his eye beneath his most recent brush stroke.

He continued to work at it. His brush uncovering more and more of what was starting to look like a short sword or dagger. The handle was cleared first. It had a metallic studded button on top above the remains of, what looked to be a leather bound handle. Then a collar that matched the buttoned top. Steve continued to brush clear the earth. He was excited at his discovery as he cleared more and more of the weapon. It was obvious now that it was indeed a dagger. It had a twenty centimetre, double sided blade, when it was uncovered. Steve could not believe the condition of the weapon. Apart from the decaying leather handle grip, the knife looked almost new.

Steve stood and looked back towards the tents to see if his father and the professor were on their way back. They were still in the tent; Steve's father was bent over the table obviously discussing some point with the still seated professor. Steve waited for a moment, but to him it seemed like ages. Still his father and the professor had not made a move. Eventually Steve's impatience got the better of him. He bent down to pick up the dagger.

A searing pain ran, first, through Steve's right hand, then along the length of his arm before culminating into what felt like a massive electric shock in the centre of his back. The force of the shock caused Steve to drop, blinded, to his knees and for a moment Steve did not move. The pain ached through his whole body as he knelt on the ground and when he opened his eyes he saw nothing, just white.

After a moment Steve's vision started to clear. Objects started to come back into focus and there was something wrong. Steve was cold to the point where he was shivering beyond control. He then noticed he was no longer at a dig site on top of a green hill on a summers evening. Instead it was snowing and he was kneeling in the snow in a clearing between buildings.

Steve could not get this through his head. He must have knocked himself out, he must be dreaming, but no, here he was kneeling in heavy falling snow. With no sign of the dig site anywhere. He looked down and he still held the dagger he had discovered. It was gripped tightly in his hand, now brighter than ever but now with a crimson tint to the blade. The snow in which he was kneeling had the same crimson tint spreading towards him like a slow tide. The red colour leaching into the pure white snow like candied ice sold at a fair ground stall. Steve watched as the red oozed further in the snow, diverted by a wooden staff lying in the snow and then towards where he was kneeling.

Then Steve lifted his head. He looked slightly ahead of himself, in the direction from where the crimson colour came. He was shocked to see the face of a young woman no more than a girl. She was maybe his age, and she was lying ashen and silent in the snow.

Chapter Eight

S teve studied the girls face for a moment. Her skin was pale and flawless. It was as if she was sleeping. Her eyes were closed but her eyelids were flickering ever so slightly. Her long blond hair was blowing in wisps around her face, by the snow filled wind. The shining glint of a piece of jewellery caught Steve's eye. It was a pin almost exactly like the one his father had discovered during the excavation at the dig site. The Odin's priest piece, although this one looked bright and new. The pin was being used to keep a heavy woollen, almost black, cloak fastened round the fallen girl's neck. Then Steve noticed the source of the crimson flow, an alien intrusion into the pure whiteness of the snow, just below the pin in the centre of her torso was a wound, a deep gaping wound. It was almost diamond in shape, from where blood still flowed. This was not like the blood Steve was used to seeing in the movies, all bright red and gushing. This was a deep crimson that flowed with a slow certain inevitability.

His surroundings started to spin and nausea gripped at Steve's stomach. He had to look away from all that blood, from that wound. Then he had to turn to one side as he lost his inner battle quickly followed by the contents of his stomach. As he retched he heard the girl try to speak. Steve turned back to see her eyes flutter open for just a moment and she looked like she was attempting to speak. Then she coughed and choked as blood bubbled to her lips and ran down the side of her face. She coughed once more and then she said no more.

A nearby scream sounded above the wind. It was almost animal like, and was heavy with a sense of rage and anger. It was a sound that immediately brought Steve back to his senses. He looked around trying to see from where it had come. Steve saw nothing, no one. Then once again the scream came louder and closer this time. It was followed by someone yelling in a guttural dialect. The words were almost Germanic, but at the same time primitive in construction preventing Steve from understanding what was said.

Looking around again Steve could still see nothing. There was no one. The snow storm and its mix of constant shifting flurries and shadows kept the owner of the voice hidden from view. Then Steve spotted it. The source of the scream, of the rage and anger. There was someone or something across the clearing. They emerged purposely either from beside, or inside one of the buildings. At first Steve thought it must be a bear, but as the figure stepped forward he saw it was huge bearded man with hair as white as the snow itself. A matching platted beard covered his face and he was clad head to foot in furs of white. He held a huge double bladed axe in one hand and a short sword in the other. Well it looked like a short sword in the hands of the huge man, but could easily have been a deception of scale. The person, the warrior for that was without doubt what he was, purposely approached Steve from across the clearing. He stood almost seven feet tall with a width across the shoulders that gave the impression that he would have to turn sideways to pass through a doorway. Steve felt fear.

The huge warrior gave another yell as his stride quickened into a charge. Another scream accompanied that of the warrior's. It was a high pitched female scream. It originated from someone who was still out of sight. The warrior's huge frame and by the constantly shifting and swirling snow storm blocked them from Steve's view. Not knowing what was going on but understanding that it was best not waiting round to find out Steve rose to his feet, ready to run.

At first Steve was still a little unsteady on his legs and the biting cold was freezing him to the core. Then the sight of the warrior, now almost upon him, convinced

Steve's legs to move. He first turned to run in the opposite direction from which the warrior approached. From the corner of a building, through the snow, Steve spotted someone, an almost familiar figure, dressed in black. The direction was therefore ruled out by the crouched, watching, presence. To the left there was nowhere to go; all escapes were blocked by what he assumed to be the solid walls of buildings. Steve span round on his heel and headed off at a dead run to the right. This was the option open to him. He hoped that this way would be open to escape.

The snow cleared briefly and a feeling of panic crept into Steve's ever faster beating heart. The direction he was heading also seemed to be blocked by the walls of buildings. Steve was about to give up hope, then the snow cleared once more and Steve spotted the dark shadows of a narrow gap between two of the buildings.

All the time he ran Steve could hear the heavy pounding of the massive warrior's footsteps closing from behind. It was now obvious that the warrior's size and that fact he was heavily armed was not going to slow him down. Not daring to look back to see how close the warrior was Steve hit the gap at a dead run. It was smaller than Steve thought and he hit his shoulder off one of the walls as he entered the darkness of the narrow passage way. It was in the nick of time, as he just avoided the sweep of a huge battle axe behind him. The axe had embedded itself deeply into the very same wall he had just run into.

The passageway between the two buildings was tight and Steve was just able, by turning himself sideways, to make his way along its length. The warrior on the other hand could not follow and he gave another cry of rage and frustration.

This heightened the fear that was already building in Steve's now pounding chest. Risking a look back Steve caught a glimpse of the massive warrior framed in the entrance to the passageway. He was retrieving his axe from the wall, as easily as it had been embedded in the snow that lay at his feet. Not knowing how far the warrior would have to go to get round to catch up, Steve pressed on scrambling frantically through the narrow gap.

When Steve emerged at the other side, he found himself alone. He stood between four crude buildings. They were timber framed and crudely walled with high thatched roofs. The opening opposite was slightly larger than the one from which he had just emerged so he decided to press on in the direction he was heading. The same choice presented itself twice more, and twice more he made the same decision. He passed between the backs of the small buildings and along narrow passageways. This way he hoped to avoid any other people that may be about and at the same time stay ahead of the towering white fur clad warrior. After passing through a fourth narrow passageway, Steve's way was finally blocked by a shoulder high wall. Just visible through the snow, to the left, a group of men dressed in a similar manner to the warrior stood with their back to him. They were engrossed in some sort of animated conversation so Steve turned right and followed the wall, hoping to find a way out.

After a short period Steve came again to a wall that intersected with the one he was following. Again it blocked his way forward, but as he looked along the length of it to the right, through the swirling snow storm, Steve was sure that he had spotted an opening in the wall. It looked like a gateway. It was maybe only one hundred metres away and so Steve quickened his pace.

His heart pounded like a drumbeat that was constantly increasing in tempo. His legs were burning due to the effort of the run. Steve made his desperate bid for the opening. Just before he reached it though, the white clad warrior appeared from between two buildings.

The massive figure blocked the way to the gate and Steve's escape. Steve turned quickly. He headed back the way he had come, and narrowly avoiding slipping in the now deep snow. Steve once again tried to increase his effort and pace to avoid been captured, or worse.

The pains that throbbed through Steve's legs now burnt like hell itself. Still he pushed himself to keep going. All the time he could hear the warrior closing, almost to the point of feeling the fur clad giants breath on the back of his neck. Steve quickly thought about trying to defend himself with the dagger still tightly clenched in his hand. Then just as quick the idea left his mind as being foolhardy, and again Steve pressed on.

The sound of the warrior grew closer as the chase progressed.

Then the group of men Steve had previously evaded were in front of him. He was almost on top of them. By the time he saw them through the swirling snow storm it was too late. They were turning, joined by another, to stop him. They were blocking his way. Steve quickly tried to change direction. Once again make for the series of narrow passageways that had originally facilitated his escape. This time though, the conditions underfoot eventually got the better of him.

Steve slipped catching his foot on something hidden under the soft deep snow, and he tripped.

As Steve fell towards the snow covered ground he saw two things. The giant white fur clad warrior starting to swing his axe in what must be a killer blow. And the knife he had been holding so tightly, now falling from his hand and out of reach. Simultaneously Steve and the knife hit the cold snow covered ground. Steve held up his arm to cover his face and he closed his eyes, as if that would protect him.

Chapter Nine

Steve opened his eyes behind his arm. It was a slow nervous movement at first. Then he looked round and realised he was in his own room. He was no longer sprawled in the deep snow. Instead the white that enveloped him was the white of cotton sheets. He was in bed. His own bed.

What had happened to the big warrior? What had happened to the axe that was about to cleave him in two? On these thoughts Steve quickly checked himself over. First he felt his head for any sign of a wound. Then he checked the rest of his body. Systematically he worked down the length of it to his feet. There was no sign of a wound of any type. He was OK. In fact, at that very moment, he felt on top of the world, but hungry very hungry. His belly rumbled loudly at this thought as if to give voice to the fact.

Turning quickly to get out of bed, Steve felt a bit light headed. It was as if he had stood up to quick. So he took his time and sat on the end of the bed for a moment. To let it pass. It was now that he noticed his mother sleeping in an old armchair. It must have been brought into his room from elsewhere in the house.

"Mam?" Steve called.

"Mam?" Once more this time a bit louder.

Steve's mother stirred in her chair then stretched like a cat that had just woken from a long sleep on the hearth rug.

"Steven." She said, "You're all right."

Standing and opening the bedroom door slightly she called down the stairs. "Steve. He's awake"

The sound of his father bounding up the stairs, at what sounded like two at a time, quickly followed his mother's call. Then his mother rushed to his bedside. She was, in quick time joined by his father, who had burst through the door at a dead run. Almost taking it off its hinges.

"You all right Steven?" asked his father.

Steve just looked at the two of them wondering what on earth was going on. Why all this fuss?

"Are you all right Steven?" asked his father again. This time with more urgency in his voice.

"Y-yes." replied Steve, "What's up, why shouldn't I be?"

Steve's mother dropped back into the chair with a murmur of "Thank god."

"What's up? Why shouldn't I be OK?" Steve repeated.

"You've been here, in bed and out cold, for four days." started Steve's father, "You were found collapsed and shivering with cold on the edge of Raveness. Luckily it was one of the volunteers from the dig that found you. She knew who you were."

"What?"

"Yes, they said you were delirious too. As if you were pleading with someone." interrupted Steve's mother.

Steve's father then went on, with regular interruptions from his mother, to tell Steve everything that had happened. He had returned to the trench at the dig site with the professor to find no sign of Steve. So his father had assumed that he had headed off home without him after becoming bored with waiting. After quickly securing the trench and its contents Steve's father had set of home himself. He had jogged to try and catch Steve up, but when he didn't and he arrived home to find Steve was not yet there he had just believed that he had stopped off somewhere or took a longer route home.

It was not until sometime later and the sky was darkening that his parents had become concerned that Steve had still not arrived home. Steve's father was just about to telephone the police when his phone had rang in his hand. It had been one of the volunteers from the dig site. She had said that they had come across Steve almost unconscious and delirious near the old west wall of Raveness.

The dig volunteer had wrapped Steve in a blanket by the time his parents had arrived. But he was still shivering and had begun to drift in and out of consciousness. By the time they had managed to get him back home Steve had totally slipped into unconsciousness.

His parents had called a doctor who had said that somehow Steve was suffering from mild hyperthermia, but there was nothing wrong with him that could explain the fact that he was now in what seemed to be a deep, deep sleep. A one from which he could not be woken. During two further visits, the doctor had again reaffirmed that there was nothing physically wrong with Steve that he could find. But Steve had remained the same for four days.

"What happened to you?" Asked his mother

"Nothing." Steve replied, quickly followed up with "I don't know."

"How did you get to Raveness?"

"I don't know." Steve replied once again.

"Let him rest." Interrupted his father before his mother could press any more questions.

"I am hungry." Said Steve

At which his mother stood and scuttled out the door calling that she would bring him something. This left Steve alone with his father who sat in the chair freshly vacated by his mother. He had a slightly quizzical look on his face, to which Steve just shrugged.

Ten minutes later Steve's mother returned with a tray. It contained scrambled egg, on two rounds of toast, a warmed chocolate pastry and a large glass of orange juice. As if on command Steve's belly rumbled once more. His mother handed him the tray and sat on the end of Steve's bed as he ate his breakfast hungrily. Steve had been hungrier than he thought, as he ate his breakfast even faster than his mother had prepared it. Though, on consideration it had been over four days since his lunch at the dig site.

When he had finished his mother took the tray and looked as if she was just about to ask another question, when his father intervened.

"Come on Jane. Let him Rest."

His mother and father both stood. His mother from the foot of the bed and his father from the armchair and left. With the room now empty, Steve was alone with his thoughts. He had decided, for now at least, to keep his experience, whether real or otherwise, with the dead girl and the warrior to himself. He had been found in a delirious state after all. Had it been another dream he had come up with in his delirium? His earlier nightmare could have fuelled the whole episode. If so how had he got from the dig site to Raveness in the first place? On top of that his parents had made no mention of the dagger. He remembered finding it and he still vividly remembered the shock on picking it up. He involuntarily flexed his hand at that painful memory. Yes, he would keep all that to himself. At least until he had time to investigate further.

Steve spent three more days in bed before he convinced his parents that there was nothing wrong with him. That he should be allowed to get up. Although this did take another visit from the doctor to convince his mother. It was Friday again now. It had been a week since Steve's 'episode', as his parents were calling it, had happened. Steve was feeling full of energy; he had decided to head off to where he had been found in Raveness to search for the missing dagger. The problem was that his mother insisted, since it was his first day out of bed that he stayed within sight of the cottage. And his mother.

Later that evening when they were all sitting around the table, Steve broached the subject of getting back on with things. This he tried to do in a way as not to arouse too much suspicion with his parents.

"I'll go tomorrow and thank the dig volunteer that found me." Steve said.

"It's Saturday tomorrow. Eve won't be at the dig." Steve's father said in response.

"Eve? Is that her name?" Steve asked.

"Yes. But as I said, she won't be at the dig tomorrow."

Said his father.

"I could go to see her at home. Get her some chocolates or something." said Steve.

"That would be nice." said his mother.

"OK." said his father, "We can drop you off. We have to do the shopping anyway."

Steve smiled to himself. It always took his parents ages to do the shopping. He would have at least two hours to himself so he could search for the dagger.

Chapter Ten

Steve rose early; he had not really had much sleep anyway. The anticipation of trying to find out what had happened to him kept his mind far too active for sleep. So as soon as it was reasonably acceptable he was dressed, downstairs and heading for the kitchen. His mother was already there and had started preparing breakfast. As he walked in the door his mother immediately turned and started making a fuss.

"Are you ok Steven?" she started. "Are you not sleeping properly?"

"Mam! I'm OK." Steve replied. "It's a nice day so I thought I'd make the most of it. That's all."

Steve's mother looked at him quizzically. He didn't think she totally believed him, but eventually she turned back to the stove all the same. Steve sat at the table just as his father entered the room. He kissed his mother on the cheek and then turned to Steve and made and attempt at a joke, of Steve wetting the bed, due to the fact he was up so early. At least he hadn't made a fuss like his mother thought Steve.

Almost immediately Steve's mother brought over breakfasts of scrambled eggs on toast and mugs of tea.

"No orange?" Steve asked.

"No," replied his mother, "I said last night that we need to do the shopping."

"Oh, yes." Steve replied, trying to sound disinterested.

After they had finished and cleared away the breakfast dishes, Steve stood leaning against the table waiting for his parents. They took forever dithering about, doing nothing in particular. Well that was what it seemed like to Steve.

"I thought we were going in to town?" asked Steve

"We are." replied his father, "What's the rush?"

"Nothing," Steve answered, "I just don't want to waste the whole day."

To which his mother just tutted while she continued with whatever she was doing to the cooker. Eventually they were ready. Steve's mother had taken off her apron and his father had finally pulled on his shoes. And after searching frantically for his wallet and car keys they turned to leave the cottage. Just as Steve was about to leave, he reached up and grabbed a light jacket off the coat hook.

"Why do you want that?" asked his father.

Steve stumbled for an answer. He did not want to say that he wanted to be ready in case he encountered any snow on his travels. After all he didn't want to appear to be on the wrong side of the sanity line.

"It's going to be another hot day." continued his father.

"I like it. It's cool." Steve finally replied.

Steve's father just gave him one of his looks and shook his head before locking the cottage door.

The drive to Raveness only took ten minutes or so along the quiet country roads and they were soon pulling into the car park of the Co-Op. It was the only local supermarket of any size in the coastal fishing village. When they were all out of the car, Steve's father took out his wallet, opened it, removed a note and passed it to Steve. Steve looked at it surprised that it was a twenty pound note.

"What's this for?" Steve asked.

"Well," said Steve's father, "If you are going to get Eve some chocolates and flowers, you may as well make them decent ones."

"Yeah, thanks dad." said Steve turning to leave

"Wait!" said his father.

Steve stopped and turned back to face his mother and father.

"You will need to know where Eve lives. Wont you?" Steve's father said.

"Oh yes." Steve answered, somewhat embarrassed.

Steve's father went on to methodically, and in detail, explain how to get to Eve's house. This was basically just along the old wall near the point they had entered the village. Number twelve, but being the way he was, he had to explain all this twice before he was happy that Steve wouldn't get lost.

When his father was finally through, Steve shot off to the shop. Just in the entrance there was the usual display of flowers, magazines and confectionary, Steve grabbed the first bunch of flowers that looked half decent and a small box of milk chocolates before heading to the ten items or less checkout to pay. He had been so quick that he was almost through the checkout before his mother and father had entered the shop. Steve noticed that they had a large shopping trolley rather than just a basket, or even a small trolley, and was quite happy that he would have at least two hours while his parents did their major shop.

Steve quickly made his way to the street by the wall that his father had told him Eve lived. Coincidently enough called Old Wall Street. He made his way along as the brass numbers above the doors counted up from one.

Number twelve Old Wall Street was typical of the rest of the cottages in the street. It was well kept, complete with climbing roses and a small picket fence. Steve paused a moment then knocked at the door.

Will Hogarth

At first there was no answer and Steve was about to turn around and leave. Then finally he heard the removal of a chain and the turn of the latch from the other side of the door. The door opened to reveal a slightly build young woman wearing a dressing gown and Garfield slippers. Her hair looked as his mother would describe, as if she had been dragged through a hedge backward, obviously she was fresh out of bed.

"Hi, I'm sorry for waking you. I forgot it was still early." Said Steve, as the young women looked at him as if trying to comprehend the fact she had been knocked out of bed.

"W...What?"

"I'm ..."

"Steven Thyme." she finished, as if she had just woken from a dream. "I'm Eve. It was me that found you last week. Come in, what can I do for you?"

"Well, I've come to thank you." Steve replied. Then he remembered the chocolates and flowers in his hands. "These are for you." He added thrusting the gifts forward, with a slight colour of embarrassment appearing in his cheeks. "Thank You."

"No. Thank you. You shouldn't of." Eve replied.

Steve smiled, still slightly embarrassed.

"Sit yourself down." Eve said, indicating a stool next to a breakfast bar. "Can I get you a coffee or something?"

"A tea would be nice. Thank you."

Eve busied herself in the kitchen for a few minutes then returned with a tray containing two mugs, a steaming tea pot, a sugar bowl and accoutrements. "I prefer a mug over silly cups any day." She said as she sat opposite to Steve.

"How are you feeling?" Eve asked. "Better?"

"Much thank you. I still don't know what happened though."

"No?"

"I'm hoping you can help me piece things together."

"I don't know how. I was on the way home and I found you next to the old wall." Eve Answered. "You were mumbling in the same way someone half-awake from a dream may. Then you seemed to drift back off in a similar manner. Other than that I can't tell you much more."

"Where was it you found me?" Steve asked, followed by "Did I have anything in my hand?" Thinking about the golden dagger.

"No, just you. As I said, up by the old wall."

"Can you show me?" Steve Asked.

"Hold your horses." Eve Responded. "Let me finish my tea and I'll get ready and take you.

"Thanks."

The tea seemed to take ages to drink. Steve sat making small talk, trying not to look too impatient, when finally Eve stood up.

"I can see you want to go. Give me five to get some

clothes on." Eve stood and left the kitchen.

A few minutes later Eve returned dressed in blue jeans, a yellow vest top and trainers, though her hair still looked like she had been dragged through a hedge backwards. Noting Steve's look, Eve simply stated, "It's a new style." then turned to leave, with a "Come on then." directed over her shoulder to Steve.

It only took a few minutes to walk the distance from Eve's house to the old wall. Then only a minute or so before Eve stopped, and simply stated. "Here!"

"This is where you found me?" Steve checked.

"Yes." Eve replied, "Just here .This side of the wall hands outstretched towards the collapse." She indicated to where a section of the old wall had crumbled from age.

Steve looked round for any sign of the dagger. Why should it be here he thought. It had been a week since he had been found here, and it had been snowing when he had dropped it.

"Everything OK?" Eve asked.

"What? Oh yes." Answered Steve, "I'm just trying to remember what happened."

"Are you going to be OK? I have places to go and people to see."

"Em, yes. I'm going back to meet my mam and dad." Steve replied, not to convincingly.

"Well, if you're sure. I'll see you round."

Steve didn't reply as Eve turned and left. He was

already studying the ground trying to work out what had happened to the dagger. It was some time and a lot of searching before it occurred to Steve. The wall was tall and solid when he had fallen. There had been no collapse. With this in his mind Steve moved to the rubble that had once been the wall and started moving the stones. He started with smaller ones first having to displace earth and plants as he went. The wall had obviously collapsed a long time ago. Then he moved the larger ones.

While he worked a number of people looked at him, as if he was not totally right in the head, but no one stopped him, or even interrupted. He soon cleared the rubble in front of the collapse, but found nothing. No dagger. Not even a trace.

Steve was just about to give up and leave when he thought he saw something out of the corner of his eye. He looked again and there was nothing. Then he saw it again, a glint as something metallic caught the sun. It was not on the ground where he had cleared, but in a crack in the wall behind where he had cleared. It was between two layers of stone.

Crouching down Steve checked out what he had seen. Could it be the dagger? If it was, this meant he wasn't losing his mind after all. There was defiantly something there and it was defiantly golden but it was also well covered in moss and other debris. Steve went on to pull clear the debris, to pull the object free. Then he thought twice about it. He didn't want a repeat of the last time he had handled the dagger. Steve reached out gently to touch the object with his fingertip. He was ready to snatch it away as soon as he sensed anything wrong. In fact so ready that he snatched his hand away three times before he got up the courage, but finally he touched it. Nothing happened, it was cold and metallic. Beyond that there was no shock, nothing.

Steve worked at the embedded object gradually working in loose, until he could finally get his fingers around it. Steve gave a tug but it refused to give. He worked at it a little more. Then he tugged again. This time it came free and it was the dagger. It looked exactly the same as it had when he had first found it at the dig. Steve deduced that when he had fallen and the dagger had flew from his hands that it had embedded itself in the wall. It had remained there undiscovered ever since. All well and good thought Steve, but that didn't explain the snow, the warrior or even how he had ended up in the village when he'd been at the dig site. All questions for later. At least the dagger was real. He carefully put the dagger in his inside jacket pocket and went off to find his mam and dad.

Chapter Eleven

Once back at the cottage Steve went straight up to his room.

"Are you all right Steven?" his mother called.

"Yes mam. Just going to my room."

Steve shut his bedroom door, sat on his bed and took out the dagger to examine. He knew he should really take it to his father but Steve wanted to learn more himself first. He examined it carefully, turning it over in his hand. He even held it like he was attacking an unseen foe, Other than an unnaturally cold feeling, nothing.

The cold feeling, Steve recalled experiencing before, but not with the dagger. He couldn't remember when or where exactly but he knew it was recently and here at the cottage. Beyond that it evaded his recall, an annoying memory just out of his reach.

Just then he heard footsteps on the stairs. Just as his door opened Steve stuffed the dagger back in his pocket.

"Come on Steven." his mother said, "I've been shouting for you. Lunch is ready."

"Sorry mam. I was miles away."

Steve ate his lunch without even noticing what it was. His mind was elsewhere. Twice his mother had asked if he was alright before his father had reassured her with a gentle hand on her arm.

They all stood to leave the table and Steve turned to go back to his room.

"You're not sitting in on a day like this, are you?" Steve's father asked.

"N...No." Steve replied. "I'm just going to get changed."

Steve was just about to go upstairs when he suddenly changed his mind. Or more accurately it was like something had changed his mind for him. Instead of going upstairs he continued on into the living room. There on the sill of the broken window was the white figurine. It glowed in the muted light of the cottage. As it glowed, it radiated an unnatural chill that reached right across the room. Steve shuddered where he stood.

It was as if Steve was standing outside himself. He was watching himself walk toward the figurine. He was unable to stop himself. He watched his own hand reach out still unable to stop. Finally he grabbed the figurine. The feeling of the charge once again surged through his body. This time not as bad, but it did make him take a step back. Once again he found himself in the snow covered village.

It wasn't snowing this time. Although there was fresh snow on the ground and the wind whistled in gusts between the buildings. Glad of the fact that he still had his jacket on, Steve pulled it closed and zipped it fasten.

Steve realised that he couldn't just stand there and wait to be discovered. So set of in an attempt to get his bearings. Then no sooner had he set off and was just about to round the first corner, he collided with someone moving at speed, coming from the other direction. The momentum of the other person along with the shock was enough to upend Steve and send him sprawling in the snow.

Steve's first thoughts were ones of fear and panic. He lifted his arms across his face. It was an instinct in a way of protecting himself. He expected to be attacked at any moment. Instead a hand grabbed Steve's wrist and lifted him back to his feet.

The person that had run into Steve and then subsequently lifted him back to his feet was a young man. He was no more than early twenties. He was shorter than Steve, standing only as high as Steve's shoulder, although he did have a much more athletic build. His face was sharp almost angular, framed by neat, jet black, shoulder-length hair. An equally neat and close cropped beard complimented this. Steve was just

Will Hogarth

about to thank the stranger when with no more than a puzzled look at Steve; he turned and continued on his way. Steve watched him leave clutching at his belt almost absently and increasing his pace. Soon he was round the next corner and out of site.

Steve set off again, with a desire not to end up in trouble and a perceived need to find his way to the wall. Hopefully he could find his way to the point he had fallen last time. This time though, he took more care. After walking around the maze of buildings it became evident, even to a non-outdoors person like Steve that he was actually at the opposite end of the village from where he had been on his last visit. Away from the wall he was making for. Armed with this vital piece of information Steve turned and started making his way back through the maze of buildings and livestock pens. He kept to the back alleys where he could. He thought it best if he avoided contact with others going about their daily business.

It was down one of these back alleys that Steve came across, what could be loosely described as, a black cloak hung over a small fence. Checking he was not being watched, Steve grabbed the cloak and wrapped it around himself. The purpose of this was twofold. Firstly to provide extra warmth on top of that provided by his thin jacket. Secondly it would help him blend in a bit more. Steve had surmised that the reason for the quizzical look from his earlier encounter had been from the fact he had stood out like a sore thumb in his modern clothing.

All was going well, and to plan, until Steve emerged from one of the particular narrow passage ways that separated some of the buildings into what must have been the main market square. It was a bustling square. Even on a snow covered day like this, the open area was filled with stalls and people. They were all busy haggling over the wares on display. Steve quickly sank back into the shadows and was about to return from where he had emerged, when the sound of booming laughter caught his attention. There next to one of the stalls and leaning casually on his huge twin bladed axe was the warrior who had had chased him. The giant that had tried to kill him. Steve froze, the fear pounding in his chest and reverberating through his whole body, down through his legs and routing him to the spot.

It was then when a door, in the building to Steve's left, opened and a small feminine voice called out. "Ragnar?"

The door had opened outward and towards Steve so his view of the owner of the voice was blocked. Once again they called out in an almost musical melodious voice. "Ragnar?"

Steve's attention returned to the square just in time to see the giant warrior turn in his direction and lift his huge hand in acknowledgement. He was Ragnar; the giant that had tried to kill him was called Ragnar.

Ragnar's eyes scanned the area in Steve's direction. He had obviously heard his name but not yet spotted the person who had called him. He didn't as much look through the crowd; he more looked over it as he towered above everyone else in the square. Twice Ragnar's eyes seemed to settle on Steve and twice they moved on. Each time Steve letting out a momentarily held gasp of air. Finally Ragnar found who he was looking for and a broad toothy smile spread across his face.

The door beside Steve closed and a diminutive figure stepped forward. She held a wooden staff lightly in her right hand and a long black winter cape pulled tightly around her body. She had blond hair, which blew in a dance on in the winter breeze. It was her. It was the girl that had bled to death, lying in the snow, in front of him. Steve's mind spun. 'How could this be?'

By now Ragnar had made his way across the square to where the girl now stood. He briefly dropped to one knee then quickly rose and embraced her in an almost fatherly show of affection.

"Thorunn." Ragnar said softly before stepping back.

The fear that had routed Steve to the spot had started to pass and he was now able to step back into the narrow alleyway where he stood and watched. His mind was awash with confusion, questions and the realisation she was still alive. It was definitely the same girl that he had seen die. He had witnessed her dying gasp bubble bloodily to her ashen lips, but here she was, very much alive.

Steve was now out of ear shot of the unusual couple. For that is what they were an unusual looking couple he was a giant of a man, a formidable looking warrior and she was a slight young girl that stood not much higher than his waist. There they stood, talking animatedly, laughing and joking together, before eventually moving on.

In the short period that Steve had been engrossed in Ragnar and Thorunn it had started to snow. It was quite heavy now and was accompanied with a sudden drop in temperature. This was all that had been required for the square to clear of traders and customers alike. Only a couple of traders remained and they were feverishly packing away their stall. So Steve took the opportunity to step out from his hiding place. He started to follow Thorunn and Ragnar out of the square. His curiosity had gotten the better of his fear and he needed to know what was going on.

Chapter Twelve

Tracking, following and keeping someone in site was an art form where Steve's skills were sadly lacking. Keeping a safe distance and trying not to be spotted was not, at all as easy as Steve had expected it to be. It was nowhere near as easy as what they seemed to imply on the majority of TV programmes that he had watched. Twice already he had lost his footing and fallen in the snow. Both times he lost sight of Thorunn and Ragnar by the time he had managed to get back to his feet, but at least he had managed to quickly find them again on both occasions. Although the second time, when he quickened his pace to try and catch up with the two of them he, once again, almost collided with the same person that had knocked him off his feet earlier. The only way avoided being seen and recognised was by a quick change of direction. Only then to walk round a corner and step out, in plain view, directly in front of Thorunn and Ragnar and had to immediately retrace his last few steps. Somehow though, he had so far managed to follow them. Steve thought this was more through good luck than skill but he managed to stay hidden from their sight.

While Steve had been trailing Thorunn and Ragnar the wind had picked up substantially. It was now starting to blow, ever stronger and with more anger with each progressive gust. The snow was falling in an almost whiteout blizzard, a hurricane of ice and snow stinging Steve's face with its ferocity. At times it almost totally obstructed views in all directions.

Steve continued on and rounded another corner, but the weather conditions were making it almost impossible to see those he tracked. Any footprints were quickly covered over. Almost as soon as the impressions had been made they were gone. Ever deepening snow hid them from view. If Steve wanted to continue with following Thorunn and Ragnar without losing them, he realised with reluctance, that he could no longer both keep his distance from them, while at the same time be sure he was still on the right track. So he took a calculated risk of moving closer to try and keep them in view. He hoped that the snow storm would provide him with adequate cover to keep him hidden. As to tell the truth he thought, he was terrified of Ragnar.

Even as Steve moved closer, Thorunn and Ragnar slipped in and out of the range of his vision. At times they appeared like dark shadowy ghosts blurred by the storm. Then almost as suddenly, they were gone. They were swallowed up by an almost blanket of falling snow.

Steve continued to struggle on like this, through the storm, for what seemed to be an age. Though in reality he knew it would have only been a few minutes. His head was now pounding under the effort of constantly straining his eyes trying to keep the two of them in sight combined with the bitter cold. When all of a sudden, outside of a large building, in what must have been the centre of the village, they came to a stop.

A short conversation, that Steve could not hear properly or understand what he could hear, took place between Thorunn and Ragnar. This time there was little sign of the joviality of their earlier meeting in the market square. This time the conversation looked much more serious and considered. When they had finished talking, Ragnar once again dropped to one knee and bowed. Thorunn turned and tapped lightly at the door. She waited for a short while. Then tapped once more. This time she called out "Völva?"

After a short wait the door slowly opened. A frail old woman stepped forward and into the bleak winter's night. She was slightly taller than Thorunn but still slight of build. She wore a long blue cloak, hemmed with three bands of jewelled stones. Three strings of jewels woven, intricately, into her platted hair, which was grey with age, complimented the cloak. Finally Steve noticed that she too was leaning on a staff. It was almost identical to that of Thorunn's; with the exception that this staff was topped off with what looked to be a cap of brass and jewels.

The two women briefly exchanged looks then embraced. Thorunn once again repeated what Steve took to be the old woman's name "Völva" but this time with more than a hint of reverence to the old woman. Thorunn spoke in a way that conveyed a deep level of unquestioning respect for the old woman. It was only then that the old woman glanced at Ragnar. It was a look that was clear to Steve that indicated that the warrior had been dismissed. She then, accompanied by Thorunn, turned and went back inside the building.

For the briefest of moments, before they disappeared from sight, Steve was sure that the old woman had looked over in his direction. Not just in his direction but at him. Into his eyes. He dismissed this thought as quick as it had appeared. The old woman, this 'Völva' turned away before vanishing from sight, not even breaking her stride.

It was only after the door had finally closed that Ragnar rose to his feet. He then dusted away the wet snow clinging to his knee. Ragnar stood looking at the door for a moment. It was as if he was deciding what he should do. Then, just as a layer of snow started to build up on his massively broad shoulders, he turned away and without a sound strode off across the square.

Now faced with the choice of waiting to see if Thorunn re-emerged from the large building or following Ragnar, Steve dithered. Only for a moment though, before he set off after Ragnar. Once again almost tripping over his own feet in the suddenness of the decision. After all it was far too cold to stand around.

It did not take Steve long to catch back up to Ragnar, close enough to follow him around the perimeter of what Steve realised was another square. As Steve watched Ragnar pulled his furs close. Then he tried to shelter from the worst of the weather by using the cover afforded to him by the building for protection. Ragnar came to a stop outside the door of a long squat building. Flickering light streaming out of its many small windows. As Ragnar opened the door it became evident to Steve that this building must be some sort of tavern. When the door opened it allowed not only the light, but also the sound of raucous drunken laughter and the smell of stale ale to escape its warm confines.

After Ragnar had entered the building, Steve stood in the cold and watched. He continually shuffled his feet and rubbed his hands together to try, in vain, to keep warm. He watched the door for around ten minutes or so before coming to the conclusion that no one else was going in and no one in their right mind would be coming out any time soon. Not into this weather. Only idiots would be outdoors in a snow storm like this.

With this in his mind, and Thorunn and Ragnar now indoors for the night, Steve was feeling like one of those idiots. He decided to resume his original plan and search for the wall. He once again set off around the perimeter of the square in the same direction he and Ragnar had been heading.

He had traversed the square to a point almost opposite the tavern. It was then Steve realised where he now was. It was the square where he had first arrived in this winters landscape. It was the very same square that he had found Thorunn on the verge of death. Where she had drawn her last breath. One thought exploded into Steve's mind. This had to be why he was here for a second time. Why he had arrived in a time before the murder had happened. He was here to save her. He could save Thorunn. At first Steve panicked at the thought. He tried to get his bearing in the snow storm. He tried to work out where the building was that Thorunn had entered was located. His eyes darted back and forth. He scanned each building in turn through the snow. He knew it had to be close. Then he fixed upon the door where Thorunn had entered with the old woman. It was almost diagonal to where he was now standing. Steve was just about to head off, across the open square and into the blizzard, when a sudden flash of blinding light stopped him in his tracks. A thunder clap that caused the air to almost vibrate followed the flash. It emanated from the very centre of the square. The sheer force of the explosion caused Steve to drop to his knees where he stood. He then scrambled backwards to the safety of a nearby wall. Half hidden behind the corner of one of the buildings, he faced onto the square. Steve tried his best to see what was happening within the storm.

Looking towards the centre of the square; Steve's view was obscured by a combination of the still bright afterglow of the initial flash of light and the whiteness that was the blizzarding snow. Eventually the glow subsided and through the swirling gusts of snow Steve could start to see. He could make out a figure in the centre of the square. It was kneeling down in the snow.

Steve adjusted his position. He struggled to see more clearly. The snow kept obscuring the figure from his eyes. Then the snow cleared and Steve was staring at a figure in jeans and a white t-shirt kneeling over something. A body. He was seeing himself as he had arrived in the village the first time. Watching as he knelt over the body of Thorunn.

Steve yelled out, as loud as he could. He tried to warn himself of what was about to happen, but his voice was lost. The wind and storm swept it away. He looked on, helplessly. The events unfold exactly as he remembered. The door of the tavern burst open. Ragnar, the giant of a warrior, stepped out. He had obviously been, as Steve now realised, roused by the explosion of Steve's earlier arrival. Steve once again heard the almost primeval screams of rage. He watched as the earlier version of himself searched desperately for an escape route. This including looking directly at himself as he now watched crouching from the corner of the building. Then he watched his earlier self; take off to the side of the square at a dead run. Steve realised when that had been the earlier version of himself running for his life, on that first visit to the village, the figure in black blocking his way behind had been himself, now. Then the earlier instance of himself was gone. Quickly Ragnar followed in close pursuit.

Why hadn't Steve realised earlier that he had come back to a time just prior to his first visit. He had been given a chance to save Thorunn and he had failed. She still lay there in the cold wet snow and in a pool of her own blood. She was dead. As the massive realisation of this hit him, Steve sank back into the buildings deep shadows. He sank to his knees. It was there in the now deep snow Steve sobbed into his hands. He had failed.

Chapter Thirteen

It only took a moment for Steve to regain his senses after what he had just witnessed. Realising what he needed to do, he almost instinctively leaped to his feet. And narrowly avoided slipping back over into a heap. He set off at a run. This time almost parallel to the route his earlier self would now be taking. He may have failed in the opportunity to save Thorunn; he was determined not to miss the chance to find out what had happened to himself. He needed to know what had happened in those last few minutes of his earlier visit. Had a blow from Ragnar dispatched him? Or was it something else that had caused his blackout, his episode as it was been referred too?

It didn't take Steve as long to make his way to the wall this time round. He knew where he was heading. He knew where his earlier self would end up. Plus he didn't have to contend with all the twists, turns and redirects as he had in his earlier flight, trying to evade the revenge focused Ragnar.

In his haste to get to the wall though, Steve emerged from behind the last house before the wall. It was almost the exact point where a group of men were standing chatting. He realised it was the warriors he had almost ran into during his earlier visit. Those that had blocked his way. This time though luck was on Steve's side. He was saved by the fact that he had emerged at the exact moment in time that the whole group had turned, as one, to see his earlier self being pursued by Ragnar. The sight of the giant of a warrior wielding the huge double bladed axe was enough to distract them from his presence.

Steve now stood to the rear of this group. He had his cloak pulled tightly around him, so that he would not arouse suspicion from any casual glance in his direction. His common sense screamed from within, telling him to get out of there while he had the chance. To save his neck, but the need to know what had happened was greater to the point that squashed and silenced the inner voice of reason.

Although he was at the rear of the group, Steve was tall and could comfortably see over the top of these lesser warriors. It was a daft way of looking at it, but due to the fact that Ragnar was such a man mountain it made these, although formidable, seem lesser warriors. It was from this view point that Steve watched the whole terrible scene unfold.

Steve watched as the huge warrior gained ground. With every stride he caught up to his earlier self. He watched as Ragnar purposely raised the terrible double bladed axe above his head without missing a stride. And he watched as the axe switched directions at the apex of the swing to deliver the killer blow. It was then that Steve looked on as his earlier self; fell to the snow covered ground as the axe followed him down in its huge death blow arc. As he watched himself hitting the ground heavily, just before Ragnar delivered the killer blow, Steve noticed the blood stained dagger escaping his grasp. It flew from his outstretched hand. Then there was nothing but a blinding flash, as bright as day accompanied by a deafening clap of thunder. When it cleared and Steve's eyes once again adjusted to the darkness of night. There was only the axe, emended to the hilt in the snow covered ground. Ragnar held it still, as he stood unmoving. The earlier version of Steve was nowhere to be seen. He had simply vanished.

Steve staggered back towards the buildings and let out a gasp of air. He had not realised he had been holding his breath, but as the sweet fresh cold air filled his lungs he realised he must have been holding it all the time he had been watching the events unfold. He backed up further into the deep dark shadows hoping no one had noticed him and if they had, that they had not looked to closely at his poor excuse of a disguise. After a moment

Steve once again exhaled. This time it was in relief at not being discovered.

By the time Steve had calmed himself down the group of warriors with whom he had been standing had now made their way over to Ragnar. They were now all talking at once in hushed but hurried tones. Ragnar seemed to be taking no notice as he easily extracted his axe from the frozen ground and proceeded to clean the blade. He did this in an almost reverent manner, with the edge of his white fur cloak.

Steve continued to watch from the shadows almost mesmerised and frozen to the spot by Ragnar's personality. Ragnar was still ignoring those around him and now seemed to be looking around for something as his eyes searched through the swirling snow. Then his eyes stopped searching and came to rest on a small figure emerging from between the buildings. They were still partly obscured by the swirling snow, Ragnar raised his hand in a definite show of authority. All those around him became still and silent. He turned to fully face the approaching figure. The new arrival was small of build and clad in a blue hooded cloak. Those who stood around Ragnar now parted to allow the blue cloaked figure to approach. Each of them bowing their head.

The new arrival stopped just in front of Ragnar and looked up. Ragnar in turn placed his hand on their shoulder and gently squeezed. The figure in blue looked up and using their two delicate hands dropped their hood. What Steve looked upon, once again, caused him to take a sharp intake of breath. A little louder than he should have been. Steve flinched then forced himself backwards. He stepped further and deeper into the shadows to avoid detection and now as he watched. He was stood there like some slack jawed idiot.

It was as if Thorunn had shaken off death. She once again walked the earth. The newcomer stood there, still, saying nothing. She looked intently into the face of Ragnar while her blond hair blew in wisps around her ashen face.

Then Ragnar spoke. "Thorunn?"

It was a simple question to which the girl shook her head. It was an action that spoke volumes. Then Ragnar lifted his head and let out a blood curdling scream into the night. He screamed with such ferocity that all those around him, apart from the girl, took a step back. Such was the grief in Ragnar's voice. When the scream came to an end, it seemed to fill the whole night with a feeling of loss.

Ragnar was once again looking into the face of the girl. He spoke one word. "Inga." Then pulled her towards him and into a hug.

Steve closed his eyes. He tried to process what he had just witnessed and then there was a familiar voice. "Hi Steve. Are you all right?"

"W...What? Yes." Steve managed to get out as he noticed he was no longer in the snowbound village. In fact stood in the sun outside Eve's house.

"Yes Eve." he added, "Just thinking." Then he moved off before Eve could ask any more questions.

Chapter Fourteen

The next day and firmly back in the 'here and now' Steve sat alone on the grass bank to the rear of their cottage. The late afternoon sunshine warmed him as he watched down the lane, waiting for his father to return from the dig site. Steve had decided that he needed to talk things over with his father and was now almost trying to will the passage of time. As if he could somehow hasten his father's return.

"Come on dad." Steve said aloud and to himself.

Steve was trying to maintain some control over his thoughts. He tried to at least keep some level of cohesion of the order of what he needed to discuss with his father. Nevertheless, he was quickly losing that battle. The longer he sat the more his thoughts bounced round his brain like manic tennis balls. Steve tried once again to order things in his mind. He tried to work out what he would say to his father and how he would say it without sounding mad, but with little success. Instead, he gave up, lay back, embraced the warmth of the summer sun, and worked on his tan.

Steve wanted to talk to his father. Steve needed to talk to his father. Steve's father was the most logical person Steve had ever met. His father, if anyone, would be able to put all this into context. Maybe he would even be able to sort it out, be able to tell Steve what to do. Though at the same time Steve still worried about how he was going to tell his father all that had been happening without sounding like his 'episode' had affected him mentally. Without sounding like he was wrong in the head. Steve closed his eyes tightly and groaned, it just wasn't fair.

"...Steve?"

Steve jumped with a sudden start as he heard his name called. He must have drifted off to sleep in the sun. His father was now leaning over him, gently shaking him awake.

"Steve. Are you in there?"

"Y...yes dad. Sorry, I must have dozed off." Steve replied.

Steve's father smiled down to him, shaking his head and turned away towards the gate that led into the walled garden of their cottage. Steve called out.

"Dad?"

"Yes?" Steve's father answered, turning back to face him.

"Can I have a word? Can I ask you something?"

"Of course." Replied his father gesturing towards the cottage.

"No. Here in private dad. Please."

"Oh, man talk." said his father as he walked back to Steve with a smile and a wink.

Steve's father climbed up onto the verge next to Steve. He also bent over and methodically removed a couple of pebbles from the grass before sitting down next to his son.

"What can I help you with?" asked his father smiling. "Is it girls?"

"N...no!" Steve stammered. "This is about something else. Something serious."

His father just looked at Steve and waited for him to start. Then, after a while when Steve didn't say anything, his father prompted. "Well, what can I do for you? Is this to do with your episode the other night?"

At first, Steve hesitated. He did not know how to start or even what he could say without sounding like a lunatic. Then he eventually started to tell his father his story. Slowly at first and then as he progressed, faster. It was as if his tale took on a life of its own and then there was no stopping him. He needed to get it all off his chest, almost like a confession. Starting the telling of the tale had opened the floodgates.

At times while Steve was talking, he started to get

carried away. He was starting to speak so quickly that his words started flowing into one another and he had to check himself. He paused, took a breath, and then continued. Then at other times, when he remembered something that he had missed out of his tale he would just insert it into his account at the point he was at. Sometimes it made sense, sometimes not. All the time Steve spoke, his father remained silent and nodded occasionally.

By the time Steve had finished recounting his tale, he had told his father about the nightmare. Finding the dagger - twice. About the murder. In addition, recounted both of his visits to the snow covered settlement. Now Steve stood and looked at his father expectantly and on edge, but not knowing what his father was thinking or what he would say.

As was his father's nature, he did not say anything immediately. Instead, he looked as if he was considering everything that Steve had told him. He looked as if he was putting the facts in order in his own mind, from the chaotic clumsiness of Steve's mind to the perfect order of his own. During this period of silence, Steve was growing restless. He started to worry and shift nervously. Would his father believe him? Would he just laugh? On the other hand, would he put it down to Steve's 'episode' and call the doctor back out?

When finally Steve's father spoke to him, it was not

at all what Steve was expecting to hear.

"I think we need to go and talk to your mother!"

It was as simple as that and then he stood, turned on his heel and headed off towards the cottage without another word. Steve jumped up from where he was sitting and quickly caught up with his father, just as he was passing through the garden gate.

"So?" asked Steve.

"Just wait until we get indoors." replied his father.

"But what do you think?" Steve pressed.

"Wait 'til we get in. As I have said, we need your mother in on this." and with no further comment Steve's father made his way to the cottage and in through the back door.

Once inside, Steve's mother was where she always seemed to be. When they entered the kitchen, she turned and was just about to say something. Then she caught the serious look that must have been on Steve's father's face. She wiped her hands dry on a tea towel tucked into her apron strings and then sat at the table. Quickly Steve's father joined her. Then they both turned and looked at Steve. He knew he was expected to join them.

Chapter Fifteen

"I'm not mad," Stated Steve, "and I didn't make it up."

"Why don't you tell your mother everything you told me, and take your time?" Steve's father asked.

"But, dad..."

"Tell your mother the whole story."

Steve's mother was sat quietly, looking nervous waiting for Steve. Steve thought his mother must know, but how could she, he hadn't told anyone until he had recounted the whole thing to his father outside. His mother couldn't have heard from inside the cottage but she certainly looked nervous, as if she was expecting bad news. So once again Steve recounted his tale, this time with more care, more structure and more detail. He told them everything he had told his father but this time more of what he knew of Ragnar and Thorunn.

When he had finished, Steve looked down at the table not wanting to look at either of his parents in the face.

At first it did not register with Steve what he was hearing but then it was clearly a sob. Steve looked up and his mother was crying. Steve could not believe it, he could never recall seeing his mother cry, but here sitting at the table his mother was openly sobbing.

"I'm not lying mam honest." Steve said

"I know." replied his mother between sobs.

"And I'm not going mad!"

"I know you're not son."

"Then what?"

Steve's father put a comforting arm around his mother and spoke gently to her, "We have to tell him Jane."

"But..."

"We have to, I know we hoped that we would never have to, not like this, but we do."

The atmosphere hung heavy in the room while both Steve and his father looked to his mother. Then, after a moment she seemed to gather her composure and simply said "OK."

"Tell me what?" asked Steve.

For a moment nothing was said.

"Tell me what?" asked Steve once again.

"Steven," Said his father, "You, are a Time-Walker."

"A What?"

"A Time-Walker." repeated his father.

"Don't be daft." Steve replied, "There's no such thing."

116

"How can you be sure?" countered his father

"Because I would have heard of them and I haven't." Steve replied, "There's no such thing!"

"But there is, and you are one."

"But..."

"It has run in our family for generations, as far back as anyone can trace. Our name was originally 'Time' but sometime back it was changed to 'Thyme' to try and end the line, but it never worked."

"So this has happened to you? You have had episodes like this?" Steve asked, "You have Time-Walked?"

"No." answered his father, "Not me, I wasn't lucky enough to have the active gene. Or I was lucky if you look at it another way."

To this statement Steve's mother murmured and gently squeezed her husband's arm, showing that she thought the latter part of that statement was the case.

"Neither was my father," Steve's father continued, "He also lacked the gene. It often skips a generation but rarely two."

"So why didn't anyone tell me about this?" asked Steve.

"As I said the gene often skips a generation." Steve's father said "But it was unheard of to skip two, so your mother and I hoped the gene had died out."

"What do you mean by died out?"

"Exactly that. Genes are diluted as families join, so

117

we thought that the gene may have died out and you would be safe too."

"What do you mean safe?"

"Well it's not without risks." answered his father, "You know that yourself from what you have told me about being chased by the warrior, by Ragnar, that's what you said?"

"Yes."

"It is said that if you are killed out of your time than that's it, you don't get to come back. Well when I say 'it is said' what I mean is that is what we think. My grandfather, Tyler, your great grandfather, the last of the family Time-Walkers, he just disappeared."

"What do you mean disappeared?"

"What I said." Steve's father replied, "We think he was somewhere else in time and met a sticky end. He wasn't very old; my father was just a young lad at the time."

Steve sat there for a moment, trying to take all this in, then stood suddenly knocking his chair over in the process. He then paced back and forth shaking his head.

"This can't be right though!" said Steve.

"But it is." answered his father, "Your mother, I mean we, wish otherwise but it is. Sit yourself down."

Steve picked his chair back up from the kitchen floor and sat back at the table with his parents. "So," said Steve, "if I can die out of time, I'll just not ... well I'll just not Time-Walk anymore."

"It isn't that easy." replied his father, "You said that the first time it happened it was when you held the dagger at the graveside. Then the second you had the dagger and picked up the figurine, yes?"

"Yes?"

"Well in the first instance it takes an object, something from the past or something linked to the past to open the pathway for a Time-Walker. Do you have the dagger and the figurine?"

He did, Steve had been carrying them around almost without realising and he didn't know why. He took them from his jacket pocket and put them on the table. Steve's father first picked up the figurine and turned it over in his hand then replaced it on the table. Then he did the same with the dagger; and again placed it back on the table.

"These two items have opened the path that you walk between times; the path is now there for you. Do these feel strange to you? Do they feel ... cold?"

"Yes." replied Steve, "How did you know? Do they not feel cold to you?"

"They just feel normal to me. The dagger, although a mighty fine example, just feels like any other metallic object and the figurine, well the figurine is just another, But to you these were the keys to the past, the keys that opened the pathway you have walked."

"In that case," said Steve, "I'll just not touch them

119

again, and then I'll not go back."

"It doesn't work like that," said Steve's father, "Now you have unlocked the path it is yours to walk. But it only took the two objects because you are still young and it was your first time. You will walk that path whether you want to or not."

"But that's not fair." Steve said. "How do you know all this if your grandfather disappeared when your dad was just young?"

"It's all write down." said Steve's father.

"It's what?"

"It's all written down in journals. They are passed down the generation, to a Time-Walker on his first walk and to those of us that don't walk, when we reach our majority."

"Your what?"

"Our majority. When we turn twenty one, old fashioned I know, but that has always been the way."

"That must be a lot of books?"

"It is. A whole wall of the library at the summer house, your grandfather's old house."

"I didn't know there was a library at granddads."

"Yep there is. It's just well hidden."

"But if the books are at granddads how am I going to get them. How am I going to learn anything? You said they were passed on when someone did their first walk; there first Time-Walk. So how do I get them?"

"Don't worry," said his father, "It's the modern age after all, I have had them digitised. Jane?"

Steve's mother, who had been sitting silently throughout the whole conversation got up from her chair, crossed the kitchen and picked up Steve's father's briefcase from next to the coat rack. She looked grave, sad even when she returned and put the briefcase on the table. Once again took her seat next to Steve's father and latched onto his arm. Steve's dad, carefully, dialled in the combination to the single lock on the tattered brown briefcase and opened it. He reached in and retrieved the only thing that it contained, a small black folio containing an e-reader, and handed it to Steve.

"Here you go," said Steve's father, "The Time-Walker Journals."

Chapter Sixteen

"This is them?" asked Steve.

"Yes." said his father. "I suggest you start at the most recent. Start with Tyler Thymes. Although he went missing young, he was bright. He had many theories and written it all down."

Steve stood, careful this time and pushed his chair back away from the table. He left his parents where they sat, and headed, e-reader in hand, towards his room. Just as he was about to leave, he heard his mother sob. When he turned to look back his father was holding her tightly in his arms, in an embrace intended to provide comfort. Steve said nothing and quietly left the room.

Once in his room he flicked the switch on the e-reader and the screen quickly formed into the directory of contents. The ordered directory was easy to follow. What else did Steve expect of something coming from his father? The one at the top was marked as 'The Journals of Tyler Thyme' so Steve highlighted the journal, clicked and it launched. At first Steve flicked randomly back and forth through the scanned contents of the journal in an attempt to speed-read it. He hoped he would gleam useful information as quick as possible. He quickly gave up on this as a lost cause and returned to the first entry. Steve started to read methodically through the entries in the order that they had been initially wrote by, his great-grandfather, Tyler.

The first entry was not what Steve expected. It did not refer to Time-Walking. Instead, Tyler had written about been informed about his legacy. His father had sat him down at a young age and informed him that he may be a Time-Walker. This was in stark contrast to what had happened to Steve. Steve had stumbled his way through his second Time-Walk, only then he had been informed. Tyler had obviously been a bit of a scholar and applied the adage 'to be forewarned was to be forearmed' and had spent a lot of time researching and theorising on the whole Time-Walking phenomenon.

Tyler had gone as far as to document the facts, the rules even, of Time-Walking as he saw them. The first rules reinforced what his father had told him. Which made sense as his father would have gained most of his knowledge from these very same journals. These rules were to do with the fact that one, or more, physical objects were needed to originally open the pathway to the past. Then once the pathway had been open the Time-

Walk could be made at any time. Also if the Time-Walker was pulled back, there was nothing they could do to prevent it. Next to this there was a note in the margin, probably added later, after experience thought Steve.

He would be able to sense these objects, these keys to the past. They would feel either cold or as a build up of static, to a Time-Walker.

The next rule was more of a theory but simply stating that Time-Walks could only be back in time. It jumped out at Steve how logical this was as he read on. As it stated that as an object from the time period formed the key to the pathway and that we could not have objects from the future then all Time-Walks would be backward in time. There was another, later added entry in the margin next to this, but Steve could not make it out through the smudged writing so he pressed on.

The next rule was the one that hit Steve the hardest, it described how solid, known about, events in the past could not be changed. This was because we already knew about them. Tyler went on elaborating with an example of how, if we were pulled back in time to 1861, you couldn't prevent the death of Prince Albert. Prince Albert died in 1861. It was a fixed event in time. A Time-Walker could not change these fixed, significant events. This reasoned Steve was why he was unable to save Thorunn. She had been murdered, on that dark night, in the snowbound Viking settlement. She had been buried on

Ravensby Tops, and then discovered during the dig. Murder must be a significant therefore fixed event in time.

Steve sat back at this realisation and his head swam, he had so many questions. If only his great-grandfather had been here to answer them. Instead Steve needed to do it the hard way by wading through the journals. He couldn't even search, as each page was just an image scan, rather than the transcription of, the original journal page, so onward Steve read.

Steve read on through the night wanting to find the answer to the question that had now all but consumed him. 'If he could not change the past, if he could not save Thorunn, then what was he there to do?'

Night had finally giving up its battle in holding back the onward march of day. As the sun broke its early morning horizon to announce the arrival of dawn, when Steve finally found an answer, or at least part of it, to his question. They, the Time-Walkers were summoned back in time to help keep time moving in the right direction or to help a troubled soul so they could finally rest and move on.

After spending as long reading the journals on an e-screen, accompanied by now being so tired, Steve's eyes stung. Realising he could read no longer Steve laid back on his bed and quickly, despite a spinning mind drifted off to sleep.

Will Hogarth

After only a few hours sleep, Steve was woken by the smell of bacon cooking downstairs. The smell was as much as Steve could cope with and he jumped up from bed and headed down stairs, still dressed in the previous days clothing. When he reached the kitchen he realised that he was not the only one that had been up most of the night. His mother's eyes were rimmed red and bloodshot, probably from a combination of crying and a lack of sleep.

"Are you ok mam?"

"Yes, yes Steven, it's just ..."

"Just what?"

"You are going to be in danger. You are a Time-Walker and there's nothing I can do to either help or prevent it. It's a hard place for a mother to be."

"I'll be ok mam."

"Yes, I know," said Steve's mother before quickly turning to hide a fresh tear rolling down her cheek. "I was just hoping, well hoping that you would be skipped too, like your father."

After composing herself she served a breakfast of bacon baps just as Steve's father entered the kitchen from the garden, also still in yesterday's clothing. It was now obvious to Steve that the whole family had been up all night.

After they had ate Steve's mother cleared the table into the kitchen sink and joined them at the table. A major development in his own right, Steve's mother never left the dishes unwashed and benches un-wiped.

"Well?" asked Steve's mother, "You're a bright lad, what are your thoughts?"

Steve drank the last of his orange juice then recapped on what he had managed to learn from Tyler's journals. Finishing with the fact that he thought he had discovered that he had walked the time pathway in order to help a restless soul. All the time his parents, sat, listened and nodded, treating him like an adult for the first time in his life. It was as if, now Steve was a Time-Walker, his childhood had gone.

"But how do I know how I am supposed to help?" asked Steve, "What am I supposed to do if I can't save her? If Thorunn's murder is a solid in time?"

Steve's father thought on this for a moment before answering then stated simply, "You need to solve the murder. Find out who committed the crime and ensure they are brought to justice."

"You mean like Hercule Poirot or Miss Marple in an Agatha Christie book?"

"Yes, exactly like that."

"But Ragnar thinks it was me. He saw me kneeling over Thorunn with the murder weapon in my hand."

"Well, I suggest you tread carefully there." stated Steve's father, as he sat back in his chair quite happy with himself and his power of deduction.

The rest of the morning was spent discussing, in Steve's opinion, more mundane matters such as logistics and preparations. Steve's father loved to be logical and organised and therefore loved to plan. He suggested that Steve start carrying a small rucksack with a cloak and few other items of clothing that would help him blend into a pre-Christian Viking settlement. Jeans and a t-shirt stood out a bit too much Steve's father also insisted that Steve kept hold of the dagger, 'as means of protection', until this was all over. Steve's mother had started to object but quickly, and unusually, fell silent after a look from his father. It was apparent that, in the subject of Time-Walking, Steve's mother considered his father to be the expert.

Next Steve's father started on the language, "After all," he said, "You'll not make much of a sleuth if you can't understand what people are saying."

Steve thought his father was enjoying this far too much. "I thought they were speaking some sort of German, at first."

"I can understand why." replied his father, "With your grasp of modern languages, but you have to remember this is twelve hundred years ago, give or take. So it would have been an early version of today's languages. It is Viking, Dame, Norse early Germanic whatever you want to call it and it is one of the building blocks, along with French, of modern English."

The whole day was spent like this. With Steve's dad helping Steve with what he was now just calling Viking, while his mother pottered around, topping up the tea and bringing food from time to time. It was handy, thought Steve, that his father was a historian and archaeologist. This was soon accompanied by a moment of realisation, this why his family had always been historians and archaeologists. They need to be, they needed the knowledge of the past. When he voiced this realisation to his father, he just laughed, "You have only just realised that?" Their conversation continued well into the night.

Just before they retired for the evening a final question occurred to Steve. "How do I know when I'll next walk the time pathway?"

"You won't." answered his father, "When you become an experienced Time-Walker, if it is strong within you, you can choose to walk at any time between the pathway being unlocked and it once again locking. But you may be pulled back at times, you'll be forced to walk and there's nothing you can do to prevent it. Just be prepared. A good Time-Walker is like a good boy scout, always prepared."

"What do you mean by locking?"

"When you have accomplished what you have been called to do, that pathway will no longer be open to you. Your anchor to that moment in time, in this case the restless soul will have moved on. It is explained later in my Grandfather's journal. No matter what happened to him, Tyler was a bright man. I think it's him you take after."

It was late, or was it early the next day, Steve was no longer sure. All he was sure of was he was very tired and his head was as full of information as he could cope with for one day. It was with a content feeling he climbed the stairs to bed, following his mother and father who climbed the stairs hand in hand.

Chapter Seventeen

The next few days passed without incident. Steve started to carry his backpack, as they had discussed. It contained the clothes his parents had provided, along with the dagger and a map his father had drawn up. His father has explained that the map was the best he could find based on what was known of the early Viking period in this part of North Yorkshire.

Steve had handled the dagger several times. It had still felt cold, felt like, what he now knew was, a key to a time pathway, but handling it did not draw him along the path. So Steve stuffed it into the backpack and carried it round with the rest of the stuff.

Steve had tried, several times, to force himself back in time. He tried to force the Time-Walk, but had given up when the only thing to happen was that he ended up with a pounding headache. So for now life continued as normal with Steve stuck in the here and now. The familiar feelings of boredom mixed with expectation

131

taking hold of his subconscious. As a means of relieving the boredom Steve returned to reading Tyler's Journals. He was specifically looking out for any details of how to force, or choose when to, Time-Walk. Steve knew that Tyler would have worked on the same problems himself. He just needed to find the points in the journal where Tyler had documented them. Early entries on this subject just confirmed what Steve had found out himself. Trying and failing left you feeling ill, nauseous and with a headache from hell.

It was not until much later that Tyler had documented successful attempts of choosing when to walk. Originally Tyler had put these odd successes down to luck. Then he had grown more excited in his entries on the subject. With each new attempt, Tyler had been able to master 'selective Time-Walking' as he called it. Although he had called it selective, as he could Time-Walk at will, he could still be pulled into the past at any time.

Steve re-read these entries several times. He tried to sort the facts from the theories and other random thoughts. As although Tyler had been thorough and he had obviously been intelligent it became obvious from reading the journals that his brain seemed to work overtime on a dozen plus different things at once. Tyler just wrote them down as fast as his hands could keep up. Quite often his words and sentences ran into one another. A far cry from Steve's father's precise and ordered mind thought Steve.

After spending the best part of the morning extracting and organising the facts Steve was sure of several things. Firstly, you couldn't just choose to Time-Walk to any point in time. A time key had to be used to open a pathway. Then when the pathway closed you could not walk that pathway again. Also, the length of time that pathway remained open seemed random. Next as a Time-Walker you could not avoid the pull of the Time-Walk. When it pulled the walker was dragged, even kicking and screaming into the past and there was nothing the Time-Walker could do to stop it. Finally, and the fact that made Steve let out an "It's just not fair!" groan, was the fact that you needed a lot of experience to choose to walk. You needed this experience as it was only through making many walks, through different pathways, that a Time-Walker gained experience. This would enable the Time-Walker to pick out the disturbances in time that surrounded them. Then manipulate these disturbances in a way that would allow the Time-Walker to simply step through time with any level of success.

Steve was disheartened and his eyes were sore from reading and his back ached from spending as long sat in one position. He stood and stretched out, his hands touching the low cottage ceiling, until his back give out a loud crack. His mother hated it when he did that. But it felt good and worked out the creases.

There was one more thing that Steve wanted to know. The old woman, Thorunn had called her Völva, but Steve thought it had sounded more like a title than a name. So he sat at his computer and called up the search engine.

There it was Völva or Völur in plural were women that practiced sorcery, shamanism, prophesy and other forms of magic. The Völva were held in high regard in Viking society. Apparently, even Odin himself was said to have consulted their kind. These women were far from stay at home types and instead accompanied the men into battle. They foretold outcomes and weaved their spells to try an influence those outcomes. So that is why Ragnar and Thorunn had acted the way they had. The old woman had been one of these witches, one of these spell wavers.

Steve had had enough of research for the day and shut down and closed his computer and headed out of the cottage. He had already decided to go and visit his father at the dig. Maybe a chat was what he needed. Steve had not got as far as the gate to the lane when he had to run back and collect his backpack. Sods law was that he would end up Time-Walking when he was not prepared. After grabbing his pack Steve set off down the lane and towards Ravensby Tops. He was looking forward to seeing the other artefact his father had said they had discovered in Thorunn's grave. Steve was now sure that it was the grave of the young woman who had been murdered on a stormy and snowy night so long ago.

Steve climbed the path up the side of the hill towards the dig site, as he did; he once again noticed the ravens calling out and circling high overhead. Watching them caused Steve to trip over a rock half protruding from the worn pathway. It was when he stood; cursing himself for being so clumsy, that Steve first noticed the chill. At first he held his breath as he panicked momentarily, but looking around confirmed that there was no snow and he was still in the here and now.

As Steve continued up the path, towards the top, the cold grew more intense. Still no Time-Walk. As he topped the rise he spotted his father and waved. His father, who was stood by the trees, returned Steve's wave. Then Steve stepped forward into the fresh deep snow of a dark winter afternoon.

Chapter Eighteen

Steve clutched at the braded strap of his backpack almost out of instinct and for a level of comfort, more than anything else. The Time-Walk had been nothing more than a single step forward in space and back in time. This time he had arrived without any side effects or displays. There was no clap of thunder and no flash of light that he was aware of. Plus, apart from a little swimming of his head, he was fully aware of his situation.

The icy cold wind howled a low thundering tone across the top of the hill tearing at Steve where he stood. After looking around he spotted a large group of people had gathered at the point where his father had stood waving. Luckily though, unlike his father, they were not looking in Steve's direction. A multitude of flaming torches, which flickered and guttered in the wind, had been thrust into the snow covered ground bathing those in attendance in a primitive orange light. The torches provided a distinct circle of light that only intruded a short distance into the semi-dark of the late afternoon. It was highly unlikely thought Steve, that they could see much in the gloom beyond that circle of light. To be safe though, Steve made a dash to the large rock that protruded from the ground and quickly hid out of site behind it. He then pulled on the over clothing in his backpack, Steve remembered Tyler's margin note 'Always be prepared!' He also allowed himself a little smile before peering out from behind the rock to see what was going on. His parents had drilled into him that he needed to find out what was going on and solve the riddle. That was the only way to close the pathway. That was exactly what Steve intended doing. That and avoid being hacked to death by a great war-axe in the process.

As Steve looked over to the crowd of people, of Vikings as he now knew they were, they all turned to face the point where the path crested the hill. At first it was just a few but soon they were all looking towards the path. Steve's eyes followed theirs. At first there was nothing to see, so Steve positioned himself to get a better view. He needed to be able to see the last section of the path before the top. The sight of a wagon being pulled up the path came into view as Steve stood on tiptoes and strained to see what was happening.

It was not horses or any other beasts of burden that pulled the waggon. Instead it was Ragnar and three other warriors. These other warriors were almost as large and as formidable looking as Ragnar and they all pulled the open waggon up the snow covered slope of the hill. Ragnar stood out from the others, dressed in his distinctive white furs. The others wore more muted furs and skins of grey, brown and black. As he pulled he constantly spoke to the others and together they walked ever onwards while straining with the weight of the waggon. Steve could tell that only Ragnar was speaking as the breath of his words formed a faint cloud like halo around his head.

The waggon was the design of a simple two-wheeled hand cart but much bigger and more substantial than any hand cart Steve could have imagined. As the cart approached the lip of the path, the point at which it crested onto the hill top, one of the warriors on the opposite side to Ragnar slipped on the snow covered ground and released his grip. For the briefest of moments it looked as if the cart was about to break loose and crash back down the side of the hill. Steve found himself holding his breath as he looked on while Ragnar and the other warriors took the strain of the weight left by their fallen comrade. The huge effort showing on their faces, but they held long enough for the fourth warrior to recover his footing and grip. He took his share of the load and once more they moved slowly, steadily, forward.

When the waggon finally reached the top of the climb

it was pulled towards the crowd of people. More people joined those stood by the young copse of trees. Steve had been so intent on the work of the warriors that he had not noticed that others had been following the waggon up the side of the hill. It was now that Steve risked moving closer. He made a point of not getting so close that he would lose the cover the darkness afforded him. But as he drew as close as he dared, he noticed that there was someone lying in the back of the waggon. They were wrapped tightly in a black woollen cloak. Steve realised it was Thorunn, or the body of Thorunn at least. Steve was at Thorunn's funeral.

The warriors leading the cart stopped and two others from the crowd rushed forward with short wooden poles. These were placed under the handles of the waggon to hold it in place. As all but Ragnar stepped back, away from the waggon and Thorunn.

Steve edged even further forward, to the very edge of the circle of flickering light, his curiosity winning out over his fear. He wanted to get a better look at what was transpiring. Ragnar pulled out a dagger from beneath his furs, held it aloft and drove it down. Without a word he plunged it deeply into the wooden slats of the waggon bed. Next the Völva stepped forward, muttering words that were not audible, and laid Thorunn's staff, along with a small wood box on the opposite side of the waggon to the dagger. Next Inga, who now Steve had surmised must be Thorunn's sister, stepped forward and placed, what looked like, silver rings on Thorunn's toes. Then she in turn stepped back and away from the waggon. The silence from those assembled was almost absolute, the only sounds to be heard being the guttering of the torches and the wind that battered the hill. All who were gathered stood and stared at the waggon, as if swallowed up in their own moment of reflection. The silence was only broken when Ragnar stepped once again forward and held aloft a large fist sized rock.

"Behold, Thunderstone!" Proclaimed Ragnar, as he turned and faced those in attendance, showing each of them what he held in his hand.

Steve had picked up the language from his father's lessons better than he had hoped. Being a geeky natural at languages obviously had some uses thought Steve.

"To protect Thorunn on her journeys." Added Ragnar once all had seen the stone. He then laid the Thunderstone at Thorunn's head before continuing. "Here on Odin's Hill we send Thorunn on her way to serve the gods."

The crowd gave out a cheer, which built as more joined in; it was the first sound many of them had made.

"She was to be our next Völva." Ragnar continued looking towards the old woman in the bejewelled blue cloak. "As our current Völva has seen her end approaching."

Many in the crowd almost wept, a mournful cry, as one.

Ragnar silenced them with a raised hand and continued with his speech. His gaze switched to Inga, "We will need to find a new Völva, but all that will have to wait, as tonight is about sending Thorunn on her way."

Again the crowd cheered. As the cheer died away, the three warriors that had helped Ragnar pull the waggon up the hill stepped forward. They stood one on each side of the waggon and one at the rear. Then they lifted the waggon off the ground and once again the strain of their effort showing on their faces. As they held it in place, Ragnar stepped forward and nodded. First he moved to one side then the other, removing the axel pin and then the wheel on each side. The warriors then walked the waggon forward and lowered it into a pre-dug grave. All those in attendance grew silent once more.

Ragnar reached out and removed one of the torches from where it was thrust into the ground. He held the torch aloft for no more than a moment, before throwing it onto the two discarded wheels. Then proclaimed "Thorunn has taken her final journey here in our world!"

The crowd erupted in a chorus of uncoordinated noise. The men beat their weapons against their shields or on the ground and the women gave out chants. The attending warriors took up shovels and filled in the grave. Then they planted a single beach tree at the head of the grave. It was only then that the noise subsided.

The planting of the tree seemed to mark the end of the Viking burial rights and the crowd began to disperse and once again make their way down the side of the hill. Steve slipped back into the darkness and watched them all go. He continued to watch for some time as a long line of torches lit the way of the path through the natural curves of the snow covered hills and back to Raveness.

Chapter Nineteen

During the funeral, the muted light of the late afternoon had given way to the full darkness of the night and the wind that had battered the hillside during the funeral was now no more than a breeze. Steve had backed up from where he had witnessed the whole thing. A handful of torches that had been left behind at the burial site combined with the soft illumination provided by a new moon and the stars were the only light on top of the hill. So the deep shadows of the night swallowed up Steve and hid him from view. Steve had watched until all the attendees had left, finally leaving only Ragnar by the grave side.

As Steve continued to watch Ragnar visibly sagged as if all of his strength had left him. His shoulders dropped. His back rounded. Then Ragnar dropped to his knees at the edge of Thorunn's final resting place.

Ragnar started to speak as if he was talking to Thorunn. His voice much softer now and unlike when he addressed the crowd. It was much harder to make out what he was saying. Steve only managed to catch segments of whispers caught on the winter breeze. From what Steve could make out it was if Ragnar was expressing not just grief and sorrow but also regret. As if he asked the spirit of Thorunn for forgiveness. Not just once but several times Ragnar asked to be forgiven, then once more he fell silent as his grief took his voice, before he stood and finally left the graveside.

Steve's mind was at a rush with what he had just witnessed. Not just the grief expressed by Ragnar, but also the huge amount of guilt he had confessed to the ghost of Thorunn. Maybe, thought Steve, it had been Ragnar that had killed Thorunn and he now regretted what he had done. That raised the question of why he had chased Steve and tried to kill him? Possibly out of fear that Steve had witnessed his crime. Maybe he was attempting to shut Steve up before he could tell anyone what he had seen.

Just as Steve was about to step forward into the ring of light afforded by the torches, he stopped himself and realised he was not as alone, on the top of Odin's Hill as he had thought. At first it was just a movement that he caught a glimpse of in the corner of his eye. But as he looked closer he realised someone was carefully making their way through the copse of young trees. The fear that he had been discovered froze Steve to the spot. He was scared that it was Ragnar once again coming after him, murder in mind, but as he watched Steve realised that the shadowy figure was too small to be Ragnar. He relaxed a little, but he still stayed hidden in the shadows and watched.

The figure eventually stepped from the near darkness of the trees into the ring of torchlight. Steve could not see the face of the new arrival as the deep shadows of its black hooded cloak kept it hidden from view. Steve could still not make out who it was or even if it was a man or a woman.

While Steve's attention had been focused on the figure in black, who was now stood head bowed at the graveside, he had not noticed the return of Ragnar. That was not until Ragnar's voice boomed across the clearing and shattered the silence. "Philippe!"

Steve looked to the direction from which Ragnar had shouted just as Ragnar himself stepped into the circle of light. Ragnar almost shook with anger as he shouted once more "Philippe!"

The hooded figure, who Steve now knew was Philippe, stood still. His back was still to Ragnar he did not even acknowledge the warriors presence. Ragnar called out once more as he started to stride across the clearing. He had covered half the distance toward Philippe before the figure in the black cloak turned to face him. As he turned he dropped his cloak to reveal his face fully illuminated

145

in the flickering light of the torches and Steve's jaw dropped.

The figure in the black cloak, Philippe, was the same man that had rounded the corner into Steve on the night of Thorunn's murder. Now that's a coincidence thought Steve; if you believe in coincidences. Which he didn't.

As Steve watched Ragnar continued to close the gap towards Philippe with the same look on his face as that night he had chased Steve. Ragnar meant to do Philippe some real damage and as he drew closer he lifted his hand over his shoulder and rasped the handle of his huge battle-axe. Until that point Philippe had stood absolutely still, but now as the threat of Ragnar became imminent he moved. He was almost cat like. He drew open the front of his cloak and lightly grasped a pair of golden coloured daggers secured to his belt and Ragnar stopped in his tracks, a scowl etched into his features.

"What are you doing here?" Asked Ragnar, "You do not belong here. You, your sort are not welcome."

Steve pondered what sort of man could stop someone like Ragnar in his tracks. Steve had thought that anything, man or beast, would be scared of Ragnar, but not Philippe. He stood their cool and relaxed, but at the same time poised with his hands still resting lightly on the hilts of his daggers.

Philippe spoke in a thick French accent "My sort?"

"Hired killers. You kill for gold and not the glory you

will never find in Valhalla." Ragnar almost spat, the contempt showing clearly on his face.

"But did I not also love Thorunn?" answered Philippe. "Am I not also allowed time to grieve and mourn her passing?"

"Your love was hollow." Ragnar answered. "It would never have been returned. She was to be Völva."

"She could have loved me. She sent word that said as much the night she was taken from us."

Ragnar shook his head and the two of them stood, eyes locked on one another, both unblinking. Ragnar's fingers once again flexed around his axe handle but Philippe still did not show any fear and he held his ground. Steve thought that the encounter was going to end in bloodshed as the moment dragged as if time had been stretched. Then without a word Ragnar stepped back and to one side, releasing his grip on his war-axe and Philippe walked slowly past. Once more leaving Ragnar alone at the graveside.

Chapter Twenty

The encounter on Odin's hill between Ragnar and Philippe had only lasted two or three minutes at the most. But its level of intensity had made it seem much longer. All the time Steve had held his breath without even realising and he now let this out in a rush. The fear of being discovered caused Steve to step back, deeper into the shadows. This high up though, even in the light breeze no one would hear.

Steve needed to decide what to do next. Did he follow Philippe down off the hill or stay and watch Ragnar as he maintained his vigil at the side of Thorunn's grave? The friction between these two confirmed Steve's suspicions, running into Philippe was far from a coincidence.

It was a friction that would end up with blood being spilt at some time in the future. That much he was sure of. So Steve decided it would be worth following Philippe. He needed to know more about the man that made the warrior think twice. Plus, he did not think that spending the night watching Ragnar mourn would reveal what he needed to know.

Philippe had a head start on Steve and was already on his way down off Odin's Hill. There was only one way down so Steve knew he would be able to catch up, but at the same time he also decided that discretion was the better part of valour. He did not want to collide with Philippe again. Not if he could help it.

So it was that Steve set off, cautiously, down the hill side after Philippe. Caution had, indeed, been the best policy as Steve caught Philippe up much quicker than he had thought. Philippe seemed to be caught up in his thoughts. He was taking his time down the hillside and along the now well worn snowy path towards the village.

All the time Steve followed, he stayed close enough as to keep Philippe in his sight. He stayed far enough back so that he could take advantage of the shadows of the night if so needed. Several times on the journey to the village, Steve did indeed need to duck for cover in the shadows. Philippe kept on looking over his shoulder as if he knew Steve was there. Maybe though, he just had a feeling that he was being followed, by someone else, like Ragnar.

All the time on the path to the village, Philippe continued looking back uneasily over his shoulder making it hard for Steve to follow. On more than one occasion Steve found himself face down in the snow, behind a tree or bush and on one occasion even in a ditch. Against the odds though, he managed to remain unseen and in time they arrived on the outskirts of the village. Where they entered through an opening in the boundary wall. Once in the village itself staying hidden, in the ever moving shadows caused by the constant flickering of torches, was much easier. In fact Philippe's sense of unease seemed to have passed now they were in the village and he stopped checking over his shoulder.

There were a few people still out and about but most had hoods up and heads down against the wintery weather, so Steve went largely unnoticed. Even those that glanced at Steve paid him little heed. The over clothing he was wearing successfully helped him blend in, especially in the dark of the night.

Steve's focus had been on Philippe and not where they were. So he was surprised when he found himself following Philippe around the perimeter of the same square where Thorunn had been murdered. Then he almost missed Philippe turn off and out of the square. At first Steve thought that Philippe had entered the same building he had seen Thorunn enter with the old Völva, but he had in fact turned down an alleyway just before the building. Steve rushed to catch up and arrived just in time to see Philippe enter a building at the opposite side of the alleyway.

Yet another unlikely coincidence thought Steve.

Philippe lived in a house next to the Völva and next to where Thorunn had been murdered. Steve made his way down the alleyway, closer to the house of Philippe. With care he checked that there was no one around before he left the relative safety of the narrow shadowy alley where he had been hiding and emerged into what looked like a narrow lane between the houses. The lane seemed to wind off in both directions away from where Steve stood, somewhat limiting his range of vision. The lane itself was very quiet, with no one around. This was probably down to the late hour and foul weather thought Steve. There were a few sets of footprints in the snow. These along with the tell-tale debris of civilisation were the only blemishes on the otherwise freshly fallen and still pristine white snow.

Steve crept closer to the building hoping to find some way of seeing inside. He wanted to find out what Philippe was up to. Apart from the door that Philippe had entered there was only one more opening in the wall. A shuttered window high up towards the roofline spilled cracks of light into the darkness. Steve saw the shadows of movement in the cracks and strained on tip toes to try and see in. The window was too high for even Steve and he looked round for something to stand on.

A little way down the lane, to the right, Steve spotted what looked like a small barrel covered in snow. Closer inspection revealed it to be a chunk of a tree trunk, a log no doubt ready to be cut into sticks. Steve grabbed it and promptly dropped it again. It was heavier than he had anticipated. Steve checked around fearful that the noise may have brought someone running to find out what was going on. After a minute or so though, when no one had arrived, Steve went back to work on moving the log. First tipping it onto its side and then rolling it to under the shuttered window.

With care Steve stood the log back on its end and climbed up to peer through the shutters cracks. It took some time for Steve's eyes to adjust to the interior. A central fire pit and a number of torches hung on the walls lit the room. When his eyes did adjust he watched Philippe, who was standing facing the wall opposite. He then turned and passed through a door into what looked like another room and out of sight from Steve. The thing that caught Steve's attention though was not where Philippe had gone, but more where he had been. There on the wall was a long polished leather strap with five daggers slotted into six spaces. It was what was not there rather than what was that held Steve's gaze. There was a clear space for a sixth dagger. A missing dagger. Was it the space for the murder weapon? Was it a gap for the dagger that was now in Steve's backpack?

Too late Steve heard the footsteps that were quickly approaching in the snow. They were almost upon him when he started to turn. Just then someone swept away his legs from under him. Steve fell towards the ground. The log had not been that high and even though the ground was covered in snow; Steve still hit the ground hard. On impact his breath exploded from his lungs and out through his mouth in a sudden whistling rush. Almost immediately a savage kick made contact with his gut, filling his mouth with bile. As he doubled up in pain the leather booted foot swung in again, this time making contact with the side of his head, and Steve was enveloped in the dark, sweet, pain free embrace of unconsciousness. He tried to lift his head to see who had attacked him but his vision swam. His assailant followed up with a kick to the head. For Steve, all was dark.

Chapter Twenty One

When Steve opened his eyes the darkness was so overwhelming that it almost crushed the breath from his lungs. It was so dark that he had to physically check that he had actually opened his eyes by waving has hand, a couple of times, in front of his face. It was only by the second attempt that his eyes had adjusted enough to see his hand, even though it was almost as close as the end of his nose.

"Hello. Is there anyone there?" Steve tentatively called.

Silence was his only response.

Steve was lying on a cold, hard packed, dirt floor. It was dry and had a sort of old, stale smell that gave it away as being indoors. Apart from that Steve had no idea where he was. Or even more important when? Was he back in his own here and now or was he still somewhere in the Viking village? Plus how had he ended up here?

The first attempt at standing up was not very

successful. Disorientation caused by the darkness was compounded by the sudden movement and caused Steve's head to swim and his stomach lurch involuntarily. The memory of the leather boot catching him full in the side of the head came flooding back and Steve felt at the side of his face with his fingertips looking for an open wound. Luckily, apart from a tender patch beside his eye, he found none. Steve immediately and with a sudden thump sat back on the dirt floor while he tried to pull himself together. He thought about who it had been that had came up behind him and knocked him so unceremoniously to the ground and about the kick that had rendered him unconscious. It could have been any one of the individuals he had been watching or, come to think of it, anyone else in the village. Maybe it was someone that he hadn't noticed yet. Whoever it was, he had not seen them and had only heard them at the last moment. The only thing he knew for sure was that they had been very light on their feet and could move quietly, even in crisp snow.

After sitting on the floor for a few more minutes Steve's head stopped swimming and the urge to vomit subsided. Time to try standing again. This time taking his time, he got to his feet. Not wanting to bump into anything, or even trip over anything, which was Steve's habit at the best of times never mind in the dark, Steve then shuffled forward with his hands stretched out in front, zombie style. When he finally came to a wall Steve estimated that even though it had taken some time to get there, it would have been only three or four normal paces from where he had awoken. Next Steve started to make his way around the perimeter of the room, carefully feeling the walls as he went, reaching up and down, in hope of finding a doorway or other way to get out of his dark prison. After only a couple of steps, Steve's foot brushed something on the floor. Reaching down in the darkness, scared that something may grab him, he felt the familiar shape of his rucksack against the wall and felt relieved and a bit foolish. Further inspection revealed the dagger was still safely wrapped where he had left it. Whoever had left him here unconscious had, obviously, not bothered with searching him. Maybe they didn't think he was much of a threat, or maybe they just weren't bothered.

Continuing searching around the walls, Steve was now desperate for a way out but due to the darkness the search was very slow going. Several times he bumped into other items in the room, various heavy wooden barrels along with rough cloth sacks which contained, what felt like, various types of vegetables. These items seemed to fill most of the room; a room that Steve now gathered was some sort of store room, maybe a food cellar.

The thought of being in a cellar panicked Steve. If the

entrance was through a trapdoor above, Steve would struggle to find it in the darkness he had found himself. He put more effort into his task working harder and quicker. In the process working up a sweat which just added to the panic and the feeling of hopelessness that he could feel building inside himself. Soon he had completed a full circuit of the room and found nothing that indicated a way out.

Steve turned and sagged heavy against the wall. Slowly he slid down, until he was once again sitting on the dirt floor. It was useless and he did not know what to do next. He sat and hung his head into his hands, almost at the point of sobbing that it wasn't fair. Then it hit him in a moment of realisation. The wall had been colder higher up. Not just colder but very cold. That meant that the store room he was in was probably underground but may not be fully buried. The upper part of the wall could be above ground level and exposed to the wintery weather. That would explain the cold. Steve stood and started to franticly search once again. This time he moved much quicker than last time. He now knew the layout of the room, but this time he searched as high up the wall as he could, almost up to the ceiling. He had almost completed another full circuit of the room and had still found nothing. He was just about to give up when he got back to his backpack and there, above the backpack, high in the wall was a small wooden door.

157

Hope filled Steve as his dark mood once again lifted. The doorway was slightly too high for Steve to make out any more, but it was a door. Cutting across the room to where he had found the barrels. Steve tried to grab one but they were a lot heavier than he could manage to lift, but it wasn't long before he had tilted one slightly onto its lip and was able to roll it, in an 'S' like path, over to his backpack and below the doorway.

One thing Steve had realised though was that the cold meant it was winter outside and winter therefore meant he was not in his here and now. He was still in the Viking village and therefore still in mortal danger. He was now dripping in sweat but he pressed on. He didn't know when, or even if, whoever had left him here was coming back. He needed to get out. Standing on the barrel Steve quickly ran his fingers over every inch of the wooden door and around its frame.

The doorway was a little wider than the barrel he was now stood upon was tall. It went the short way up into the ceiling where it met another similar sized door directly above him. Obviously, this was how provisions were brought into the store, and how he had been deposited by his assailant. That also explained why his backpack was where he found it. Steve once again traced his fingers around the edges of both doors looking for a latch or other way to open either of them from the inside. Steve's' gut dropped, as on full inspection it became obvious that there was no way to open either. The door was made of solid wood and was a tight fit but Steve pushed at it to see if it would give way under pressure. Nothing. He only succeeded in almost pushing himself off the barrel. Steve rattled the door and listened then did the same once more. From what he could tell it sounded, and felt, like a wooden cross bar held the door in the wall secure. The door in the wall then held in place the door in the ceiling.

After some thought, Steve's mind returned to the dagger wrapped in his backpack. Maybe he could dig a hole through the door and then lift the bar free. Steve jumped down from the barrel and retrieved his backpack and the dagger. He'd just climbed back on top of the barrel and was about to start when he heard a scraping sound from the other side of the door. A moment late Steve was blinking into the moonlit exterior. His heart almost coming to a complete stop from shock. As his eyes readjusted and he looked out of the doorway onto a figure standing silhouetted in the moonlight.

Chapter Twenty Two

The silhouetted figure leaned forward reaching towards Steve, who, once again, almost fell backwards from the barrel he was standing on. Just as he was about to completely overbalance an outreached hand grabbed the collar of his cloak and steadied him. Then the newcomer spoke in a soft, melodious, feminine voice. "Boy. I suggest that you come with me if you want to see this night through."

Steve was just about to jump up when he remembered his backpack. He quickly jumped down and grabbed it, at the same time stuffing and hiding the dagger back inside it.

The woman's voice called down once more. "Come on. We need to go before someone comes and finds us here."

Quickly, Steve climbed back onto the barrel and scrambled up out of the now open door and back into the snow. Steve took a huge gulp of air. He was relieved to be free from his dark confines and turned to thank his rescuer and almost lost the power of speech. The silhouetted figure, his rescuer, was Thorunn's sister. Inga. Steve managed to eventually stammer his thanks. Inga said nothing as she turned and started to walk away. She had only gone a few steps when she stopped and looked back over her shoulder, gesturing for Steve to follow.

They made their way along the winding lane. The cellar where Steve had been imprisoned had only been a couple of buildings from where Steve had been watching Philippe. They quickly passed it by with Inga indicating that Steve should keep quiet. Then they continued on behind the building Thorunn had entered with the old Völva. Just as they were about to round the next bend Inga stopped and stepped back pressing Steve deep into the shadows. Almost immediately two warriors wrapped in their furs walked passed. Their heads were down against the weather and did not notice Inga and Steve as they stood in silence, hidden in the shadows.

When they had past, Inga once again, silently, gestured for Steve to follow. They emerged from the shadows and continued along the lane to the next building, where Inga opened the door and entered and Steve followed her in.

Steve found himself in a small single roomed dwelling with a high vaulted ceiling. A log fire smouldered in the centre of the room. Its thin wispy trails of smoke slowly making their way slowly up to gather in the roof space, before eventually escaping from a small hole cut in the roof for that very purpose. A bed covered in a mixture of firs and skins was positioned in one corner and a number of crude, mismatched stools surrounded the fire pit.

Drawing up one of the stools, Inga sat next to the fire, with her back to the door. She gestured for Steve to join her. Steve sat opposite Inga so he could get the best view of Thorunn's sister. Still not fully able to grasp how much the two looked alike, he sat and waited for her to say something. Inga stirred at the fire with a short metal poker and then added some fresh wood, small twigs then larger roughly cut logs. The effect was almost instant and the fire starting giving off heat. Steve had to loosen off his cloak and as he did Inga rose, removing her own cloak and hung it on one of a number of pegs in the wall next to the door. When she returned she hung a pot, of what looked like some sort of broth, over the fire and once again sat opposite Steve.

Steve had to say something, even if just to get the conversation going. Although he had listened to these Vikings talk and fully understood them, speaking the language was something else altogether. So he started slowly taking time to form his words. "How? Why?"

Inga raised her hand and interrupted Steve. "All in good time and one thing at a time."

"You are Thorunn's sister?" asked Steve.

"Yes we are ..." Then she corrected herself "We were twins. We have been inseparable since birth."

"So who murdered her?" Steve asked, almost kicking himself for his unintended bluntness and lack of sensitivity.

Inga paused and took a deep breath, but still answered Steve's question. "I can't imagine anyone wanting to hurt Thorunn never mind kill her. Everyone loved her, plus she was to be our next Völva." Then Inga asked her own question. "Why had you been locked in the winter food store? I saw someone throw you in there. Like you were nothing more than a sack of root vegetables."

"Who was it?" Steve answered the question with a question. "Maybe it was your sister's killer."

"In this weather, all I could make out were shapes in the snow." Inga answered and then she asked again, this time with a greater tone of suspicion in her voice. "You did not answer. Why did they throw you down there?"

Steve did not want to lose any of the trust he was building with Inga so answered as honest as he could. "I don't know, maybe it was your sisters killer and they thought that I may have witnessed the crime." Then he added, just to be totally honest. "Or it could have been someone who thought I was Thorunn's killer."

"Are you?" Inga asked, standing from her stool in

anger. Then she slowly sat again and added. "No. I know you are not Thorunn's killer. You are but a boy and Thorunn would never have been caught off guard by the likes of you."

Steve did not know whether to be offended or relived by this statement but he let out a sigh of relief anyway. If Inga had thought him to be responsible for Thorunn's murder, he would have had nowhere to run as his route to the door had been, very strategically, blocked by Inga. He now realised he would have foolishly been at Inga's mercy.

"Your accent, it is soft like Philippe, the Frenchman's" Inga stated. "Are you also from lands to the South?"

"Yes. Something like that." Steve answered, not knowing what else to say. Telling Inga that he was actually a Time-Walker, from several hundred years in her future could, thought Steve, cause unexpected results.

"So, you have no idea who could have killed your sister?" pressed Steve.

"I have already said no. Why would someone want to kill our next Völva?"

"What about the big warrior, Ragnar?" asked Steve.

"Never. Ragnar was our father's closest friend. They fought together, back to back in battle. When our father was mortally wounded in one of the battles for this land, Ragnar fought like Thor himself. He held off a horde of enemy warriors trying to save our fathers life."

"Trying?" Steve asked hungry for more information. The thought of men fighting almost hand to hand and ultimately to the death was so far removed from his safe modern life. Gruesome or not, Steve was intrigued.

"Yes. For nothing could have saved our father that day. He had earned his place and was destined for Valhalla." Inga said, almost proudly. "He rests on Odin's Hill where we have also buried Thorunn."

"But what about Ragnar since then?" Steve Asked.

"He became our guardian and protector, my sisters and mine. He looked after both of us until we reached our majority." Inga answered. "Then in the autumn, when Thorunn was named to succeed the old Völva, he became her personal guard and protector. He loved her - us like a second father."

Steve was just about to ask another question, when Inga added something else, almost absently. "Only once has Ragnar lost control of his temper. Since then he has lived the rest of his life making up for that moment of madness. It is not something that he would ever let happen again. Not after how it ended."

"What happened?" Steve asked, almost desperate to know.

"In the fury of an argument and with a single mighty blow, he killed his own brother."

Chapter Twenty Three

L eaning forward Inga's expression was almost vacant while she slowly stirred the broth, which was now gently bubbling in the pot. Steve had not realised he was so hungry but as the smell of the cooking food filled his nostrils, and if on cue, his belly rumbled loudly.

"Are you all right Inga?" Steve asked trying to cover his embarrassment.

"Yes. It's just; well I just miss my sister. We were so close. It's as if part of me is missing."

Inga picked up two wooden bowls that had been warming by the side of the fire and ladled into each a substantial serving of the broth, passing one to Steve. "Here you look. You sound, like you need this."

Steve blushed but took the bowl gratefully and gulped down the piping hot food, burning his mouth on several occasions, while Inga only picked at hers.

Inga looked up as Steve scraped at the bottom of his quickly emptied bowl. "Would you like some more?"

Steve blushed once more but still held out his bowl, which Inga refilled with a sad smile on her face.

Before Steve took his next mouthful though, he asked. "What about Philippe, the Frenchman?"

"What about him?" Asked Inga

"Well what is his story?" asked Steve, "What was his relationship with your sister?"

"That is not the easiest of question to answer." Inga replied. "So let me start from the beginning. It will best help explain about Thorunn and Philippe. As you need to know what went before to understand where things went."

It was now Steve's turn to just pick at his broth, as he listened intently to Inga's tale of Thorunn and Philippe.

Philippe had been here in the village when Thorunn and Inga had arrived. They had come from their homeland across the North Sea to join their father. He was not what they considered to be a warrior as he had no honour. But he was an efficient and brutal killer who fought alongside the Viking warriors. Philippe was said to have been a killer for hire, an assassin in his homeland, before he had fled his native France and headed north. He had arrived looking for adventure as much as to avoid those that were said to be after him.

Most of the other warriors looked down on him, as they still do. They considered anyone who was purely a killer for profit as someone with no honour. He was someone that would never be allowed to enter the sacred halls of Valhalla.

When Inga and Thorunn had arrived, Philippe had been in the village on that first day. Thorunn had been immediately and on first sight infatuated by him. She had fallen for the combination of his suave looks and his deadly persona. An infatuation that Philippe reciprocated on so many more levels, so much so that Philippe remained in the village rather than moving on looking for more adventure. In the time it took Thorunn to grow into womanhood they had grown much closer. Any time she could sneak away from their father and then later Ragnar, it would be to meet with Philippe.

Later the relationship had lead to a lot of friction between Ragnar and Philippe with threats been issued on both sides. Although mainly, there was always an uneasy truce between the two of them due to both of their feelings for Thorunn.

Then the relationship had ended abruptly in the autumn when Thorunn had been chosen to be the next Völva. The magic ran deep in her family, their lineage was long and strong and Thorunn took her responsibility serious. After that it was as if Thorunn had tried to cut herself off totally from Philippe. She tried to avoid him as much as possible, although Philippe had continued to follow her around and tried to change her mind at every opportunity. But it was to no avail, Thorunn's mind was set.

"I overheard Philippe say that Thorunn had said that she still loved him." Steve interrupted. "On the same day as she was killed."

"I don't think so." Inga replied. "It was the eve of the celebrations of her taking her new position. The whole village was set to welcome her as Völva. It was to be a time of joy and feasting."

Steve leaned forward absently scraping his spoon around the bottom of his now empty bowl. "So." Steve asked, "What will the village do now they don't have their new Völva?"

"They will choose another. Someone else with strength in the magic." answered Inga

Steve was just about to ask another question when Inga spoke, cutting him off.

"It'll be safe outside now. Safe for you to go. There will be no one around at this time."

Steve Stood fastening his cloak against the cold once more, more than a little reluctant to leave the warmth of the fire. Inga had made it clear though and had already stood and was opening the door for him to leave.

"Once again, thank you. Thank you for saving me." Steve said. "And thank you for telling me so much about Thorunn and the others."

Steve looked out into the lane, into the darkness. It

had almost stopped snowing but the sky still look full, promising of more still to come. Steve realised they had talked for most of the night and it would not be long till dawn broke. Steve stepped forward as Inga closed the door behind him. He pulled his cloak closer and set off. Steve felt a slight tingle like shock from static electricity and stepped once more into the summer sun.

Chapter Twenty Four

Steve was back on top of Odin's Hill, or Ravensby Tops as it was known in the here and now, walking towards his father, who was still stood waving at Steve. Things were in exactly the same place they had been when Steve had Time-Walked. As Steve took another step forward towards his father, the waving became more like an exaggerated sign language as his father's wave evolved into gestures, as if trying to tell Steve something in the way of a Christmas miming game. Before Steve had taken another step he realised what it was, partially from his father but also for the fact he was now very warm, he was still wearing his Viking over clothes. This may have looked strange to any of the others at the dig site that may have seen him.

Steve immediately dropped to the ground and started removing the outfit, stuffing it back into his rucksack. By the time he was finished Steve's father had covered the ground between them and now stood at his side.

Reaching down he lent Steve a hand in Standing.

"What Happened there?" Steve's father asked. "One minute you were walking over the top of the hill dressed as you are now. The next you were wearing your Viking clothes. They came from nowhere!"

"What, there was no interruption? I haven't been missing?" replied Steve.

"No, should there have been?"

"Yes! I Time-Walked again." Steve still struggled to say this as to him it still sounded like mad nonsense, but that is exactly what he was a Time-Walker. "I was in the Viking village again. This time for a day and a night."

"I need you to tell me about it." Steve's father said." Including how you got that bruise on the side of your face. You can tell me on the way home."

"Are you done for the day?" asked Steve.

By way of answer Steve's father shouted across the dig site to the professor. "Mary, I'm taking an early one. I'm going to walk back with Steve."

"No problems." Replied the professor, who then added. "I hope you're feeling better Steven."

Steve just smiled and waved and he and his father turned and started down the hillside. As soon as his father considered they were far enough away to be out of everyone's earshot, Steve father once again asked Steve to tell him about it and not to leave out any of the details. He was almost like a schoolboy with a thirst for a good story. His full attention focused on Steve. This was something Steve was not used to; normally his attention was on his work or anywhere else apart from Steve.

So Steve spent the whole journey home updating his father of what happened on his latest Time-Walk. He started with the funeral. Which Steve's father got very excited about saying how it all tied up with what they had found at the dig site and finishing with his chat around the fire with Inga. Several times during the tale Steve's father interrupted with a question or asked Steve to repeat something for clarification. This was especially so when Steve told him of how he had been knocked unconscious and locked in a cellar.

By the time Steve had finished reciting his tale, to his father's standards, they had reached the lane that ran along the back of the cottage they were renting.

"That's amazing Steven." Said his father. "I am honestly jealous of you, what you have seen and witnessed."

Steve stopped in his tracks and turned to face his father.

"But obviously you need to be more careful." His father added almost as an afterthought. "Also I think it may be best if you don't tell your mother about being attacked and locked in a cellar."

"OK."

"We don't want to worry her any more than she

Will Hogarth

already is. Do we?"

"No." Steve answered, when it became obvious that his father was looking for agreement.

When they got back to the cottage, Steve's mother was sitting in the garden enjoying the late afternoon sun and Steve's father announced that he was going to cook supper and it would be a barbeque. His father set about it, in his methodical fashion. He spent time getting everything ready for the barbeque, giving Steve plenty of time to update his mother on everything that had happened. Although this time skipping his episode of peril. Unlike his father though, his mother just sat quietly and listened until Steve had finished at times rubbing or ringing her own hands.

When Steve finished his mother still sat there quietly, looking at him, until his father broke the silence by announcing that the food was ready. The three of them sat round a small folding patio table, Steve's father, joined by his mother, started analysing all that Steve had told them. Once again this involved the asking questions. But this time the questioning was more focused rather than general and were all about Ragnar, Philippe and Inga.

"So." Said Steve's mother, "Do you think it could have been the warrior, Ragnar?"

Steve thought about this for a moment before answering. Mainly because he had just taken a large bite from his burger, but also to give it some level of consideration. "I don't honestly know. What I do know is I wouldn't want to be on the receiving end if he ever lost his temper. He could probably snap most men in two without much effort."

Then just as Steve was about to take another bite of his burger, his father came back with another question. "What about Philippe?"

"Well he was an assassin." Steve started. "And according to Inga he was less than happy when Thorunn ended things between them. Even less willing to believe it. Plus he seemed to even scare Ragnar and..."

"And what?" asked his mother and father in unison.

"Well there was a missing dagger in Philippe's collection. I'd forgotten about that as I just got the briefest of glimpses."

Steve's mother seemed to be deep in thought for a moment, and then asked, "What about this Inga. Thorunn's sister. Could she have had anything to do with it?"

"I don't think so." Steve said, "She did seem to be very upset at her sister's murder and she did rescue ... I mean help me."

Steve's father nearly fell off his chair at Steve's slip, but his mother just raised an eyebrow and did not comment on it as she continued. "I think you may have to do some more digging around. You need to get to the bottom of this and also see if you can get someone else's version of the story. It could still be anyone."

"But who?" Steve asked. "I think Ragnar may want to cleave me in two and Philippe is not a man I would want to mess with either."

Steve's mother once again became quiet, giving Steve a chance to finish his burger. Then Steve's father spoke. "The Völva!"

"What was that?" Steve's mother asked.

"The Old Völva." Steve's father said once more. "She will know what is going on if anyone does. Plus she shouldn't be too much risk to Steven."

"But she's a witch!" Steve objected.

"Steven, you know there's no such thing as witches." Steve's father said.

To which Steve just grumbled.

The three of them talked around the whole thing several times while they finished their meal. The plan remained the same. Steve needed to see the old Völva if he could.

As Steve pushed away his paper plate he struggled to stifle a yawn. He realised that even though it was still only early evening and everyone else was on the same day that they had got up on, with time progressing in the normal linear fashion, it wasn't so for him. Steve had in fact lived through an extra day and night, with very little sleep. That was unless you counted the time he had been unconscious. Pushing himself back from the table Steve said his goodnights and headed off up to his room.

Chapter Twenty Five

$\mathcal{A}$lthough he was exhausted when he climbed into his bed, Steve still struggled to get to sleep. The whole thing was a big puzzle, a puzzle that he needed to make progress on before his brain would switch off and allow the embrace of sleep to engulf him. The events of the past week or two were now spinning in his mind. Facts and questions were all of jumble. The questions that had been asked of him by others and by himself. He needed to get things ordered. He needed to be more like his father, if he was to make any sense of things.

Steve lay staring up at the ceiling and considered the whole purpose of his Time-Walking. If his purpose was to help or to bring justice, how was he supposed to achieve this? After all he was just a lad. Not even a man yet, out of his own time. It was not like he could tackle a Viking, even one of the women, head on and hope to win. Even if he did manage to track down the killer he just wasn't physical enough. It must be achieved, reasoned

Steve, by his intellect instead.

Thinking about the three Time-Walks he had now done, Steve realised that each one had been longer than his predecessor and allowed him to build on his knowledge. If this was a pattern the next walk would be longer again. He needed to work smart if he didn't want to end up stuck there for weeks at a time. Plus it occurred to Steve that each time that he had walked, it had been the same group of individuals he had encountered. As if there was some force at work. It must be one or more than one of those individuals that had been responsible for Thorunn's murder.

By the time Steve had organised his thoughts enough to relax, it was already getting light outside but he finally managed to fall asleep. He must have needed it as he slept well into the next morning.

His parents had left him to sleep late, well past breakfast, realising that he needed the rest. When Steve did wake, he felt rested and refreshed. Steve did not get straight up though as he thought he'd make the most of it. It was not very often that he was just allowed to lie in bed. While he lay there he picked up his e-reader from beside his bed, started it up and started reading Tyler's journal. He flicked back and forth through it, reading entries at random. One of the entries Steve read had been one of Tyler's experiments in 'choosing to walk'. It had been a failure but Tyler had made reference to sensing a static charge in the air where a pathway lay. This was just like what Steve had felt prior to his return to the here and now.

He was going to read more but his belly got the best of him. He was hungry and he needed food. So he reluctantly put the reader, and Tyler's Journal, down and climbed out of bed. He then dressed in his trademark black jeans and vintage punk tee-shirt before heading down stairs. When he got to the kitchen only his mother was there. His father had left much earlier to go to the dig site.

"Hungry?" Asked his mother. "Or is that a daft question?"

Steve sat at the kitchen table as way of answer and smiled at his mother. Within a few minutes she was putting a large plate of beans on toast in front of him. It was more of a brunch than a breakfast, but Steve wasn't fussed.

While he ate, Steve's mother sat in the chair opposite him, saying nothing. She just sat watching him eat. Finally when Steve had finished eating and was washing the last mouthful down with his juice, his mother spoke. "You are being careful, aren't you Steven?"

"Mam, don't worry." Steve replied.

Steve's Mother reached across the table and gave his arm a gentle squeeze before standing and clearing the table.

While his mother was busy with the dishes, Steve picked up his backpack and headed out the door. Just as he was about to close the door his mother called, but Steve pretended not to hear her and continued on his way through the garden and out into the lane beyond.

This time Steve had been nowhere near any of the Viking sites when it happened. When he Time-Walked. One moment he had been jumping over a dry stone wall, out of a corn field he had been cutting across. The next he was standing knee deep in snow in the middle of a copse of trees. There had been the tell-tale crackle of static and then he was here. He hadn't sensed the static in time to give him any real warning. It had just happened, almost instantly.

Steve ducked down not wanting to be seen and not at all sure where he was. He soon realised that a snow storm was once again raging around him, but the trees provided some level of protection. Steve once again pulled his Viking over clothes from his backpack and put them on. He was grateful for not just the disguise but also for the extra level of warmth they afforded him.

With care he started to make his way through the trees, hoping to get his bearings. He took things slowly as he knew that if he had arrived here, there must be at least one of his suspects nearby. It was not long before he was proved to be right. Just as Steve was nearing the edge of the copse he realised that he was back on top of

Odin's Hill. He was making his way through the same trees that Philippe had been hiding in during the funeral of Thorunn. Then, just as he was about to step into the open he had looked over towards the grave site and spotted two figures in the snow. Neither was large so therefore neither was that of Ragnar maintaining his graveside vigil.

Not wanting to risk being seen but at the same time realising what was going on was important, or he would not have arrived here at this moment to witness it, Steve stayed just inside the tree line. He slowly made his way as close to the couple as he could. Standing just behind one of the trees Steve could now see that one of those at the graveside was Inga, Thorunn's sister, the second figure had its back to Steve. They were cloaked and hooded so Steve could not see who it was. The direction of the wind stopped Steve from hearing what was being said. One thing was obvious though, whoever it was had angered Inga as she seemed to be arguing with the other person. In an extremely animated manner.

Steve stood and watched. He was almost willing the second person to turn around so he could see them. In the gut of his stomach he just knew that it was important but all the time they argued they kept their back to Steve. Then in a fury Inga lashed out, slapping the other person full in the face. The force was such that it turned the head of the other person. Turned it so Steve could see who it was, it was Philippe. As Philippe turned back Steve saw him smoothly grasp a dagger at his belt. Steve did not know whether to rush out and help Inga or stay where he was. As fear routed him to the spot, the decision was made for him. Steve need not have worried though as Philippe just straightened himself up and stalked swiftly past Inga. In turn she did not even turn to watch him go.

Steve wanted to follow Philippe again to see if he could learn more. He had learned so much last time, but that would mean revealing himself to Inga and he did not want to do that. He did not want Inga to think he had been spying on her. Instead he remained hidden by the tree while he watched. Philippe quickly swallowed up by the snow as he slipped away from the graveside.

Chapter Twenty Six

Inga remained at the graveside for some time. Her lips worked at words that Steve could not hear but could clearly see with the forming mists of breath in the chill air. Eventually she turned and started walking away from the grave and into the storm. Then she too was swallowed up by the swirling snow, and Steve followed.

Steve now knew the route from Odin's Hill to the Viking village, having already followed Philippe the same way. Following Inga was a lot easier as she was not nervous like Philippe had been and therefore did not keep looking back over her shoulder. For this Steve was grateful, the thought of diving for cover in the deep cold snow again did not appeal to him. The snow swirled in an angry battle of the many white flakes and from time to time totally obscured Inga to Steve's sight. It was obvious though that she was heading back to the village and heeding his mother's words Steve was, for a change, being careful.

When they reached the village's perimeter wall Steve paused as he did not want to walk round the corner and bump straight into Inga, which was the sort of thing he was likely to do. Instead he counted to ten then entered the village. Inga was nowhere to be seen. She had vanished.

Steve was dumfounded. She could not have gone that far. She had just been in front of him and here in the shelter of the village the storm did not obscure vision as much. So where had she gone? A thought had occurred to Steve, maybe she knew he was following and took the opportunity to give him the slip. Then he reconsidered, he had not taken any risks, he had stayed well back and therefore he could not have been seen. Calming himself Steve focused on the problem. Then he thought the most likely place Inga would have gone would be her home. The place she had taken Steve after rescuing him from the cellar.

Steve set off through the village doing his best to avoid its residents where he could. This was not as big a problem as it could have been, because although it was just mid-afternoon the winter storm was keeping most people off the streets. Those that Steve did encounter had the hoods of their cloaks up and their heads down against the storm. So most people did not even notice him.

Eventually, and in a roundabout fashion, Steve reached the winding lane where so much had happened the last time he had been in the village. This time he had entered from the bottom of the lane rather than the intersecting alley at its midpoint. Steve made his way, slow and with care, up the lane. Once again he kept to the shadows as best as he could without running the risk of drawing attention to himself. Firstly he past the food store where he had been imprisoned, its door bared once more from the outside showing no sign of the fact that he had ever been there. Then Steve crept past the home of Philippe. Even though the building was in darkness, Steve did not want to disturb him. His many questions about Philippe would have to wait for another time.

Once passed Philippe's, Steve continued up the lane towards the building Inga had taken him upon his rescue. He did not know what he was going to do, whether he was just going to watch from a distance or even if he would be brave enough to knock on the door. All he knew at that moment was that was where he was heading.

Then before he reached his intended destination something distracted Steve. He was now behind the building where he had seen Thorunn enter with the old Völva on the night of her murder. He could hear raised voices from within. The detail of what was being said was lost due to the muffling effect of the building, but he was sure that one of the voices was that of Inga.

Steve made his way down the alleyway to the square and to the front of the building in an attempt to see if he could find out what was happening. He was unexpectedly rewarded by an open shutter from which he could clearly hear and see what was going on.

Inga was standing with her back to Steve, facing the old Völva and they were arguing in a highly vocal manner. Steve checked that there was no one around that may see him. When he saw the square was deserted, he moved closer to the window and positioned himself so he could both get a better view and hear what Inga and the Völva were arguing about. Just as Steve took his position and looked back into the window the Old Völva looked over Inga's shoulder and straight at Steve. Thinking he had been discovered, Steve just looked straight back at the old woman, but she did not acknowledge seeing him. It seemed to Steve like she was looking straight through him and not seeing him at all. Maybe thought Steve that her eyesight was poor. After all she was old, and she had not seen him.

The old Völva's attention returned to the argument with Inga. In his brief moment of panic Steve had missed Inga's question but the Völva's answer was an angry "No. Never!"

"You'll not have a say in matters." Inga argued. "Your influence in this village is fading."

"I'll tell you the same thing I told your sister." Replied the old Völva, "You will never replace me as Völva. I will do whatever it takes to prevent it. Never do you hear me?"

Inga took a sudden step forward and Steve thought she was going to attack the older woman, but at the last moment the Völva raised her staff in front of her. It was not as to threaten Inga, more as to act as a shield and Inga stopped in her tracks. It looked as if she was struggling against some unseen force, trying but failing to make any progress forward. Eventually Inga relented and the Völva lowered her Staff. Inga spat and turned to the door. Steve just managing to duck before he was spotted. The door clashed open with Steve behind it, only the deep snow stopping it hitting him and knocking him senseless. Inga was obviously so enraged by her argument with the old Völva that she stormed off without shutting the door, leaving Steve hidden where he stood.

After a moment Steve heard slow, but steady, footsteps approaching the door from the inside. The Völva, Steve assumed coming to close the door and lock out the winter weather. Steve remained hiding where he stood, holding his breath and waiting to make his getaway and continue his pursuit of Inga. But the door failed to close as expected. Steve was now suspecting that he had been discovered and started to panic. Should he stay hidden or should he make a run for it. He had decided and was just about to make a run for it, after all she was an old woman and it was unlikely that the old Völva would be able to catch him, and then she spoke.

"Well are you going to let an old woman catch her death or are you going to come in Steven?"

Steve nearly died on the spot. Not only did she know he was there, she also knew what he was called. Steve stood there, behind the opened door a short while longer, and then leaned forward looking round the door at the old woman leaning on her ornate wooden staff.

"Well?" asked the Völva.

Stepping fully from behind the door, Steve entered the house, not taking his eyes from the old woman as she pulled the door closed after him. Steve looked around and found himself in a building much the same as the one Inga had took him too after freeing him from the cellar. The main differences were the size, this was a much bigger building, plus instead of a single bed in a corner, this building had continuous low, wide, benches down the length of the two longest walls. Both benches were covered in an assortment of furs and other animal skins. The fire, which sat in the centre of the room, had a metal tripod over it from which hung a large cast iron pot. Steve thought it looked very like a witch's cauldron but kept the thoughts to himself. Within it a deep red sweet spicy smelling liquid gently simmered. The fire was low but still gave off ample heat to warm the large room and the small amount of smoke it produced, drifted slowly upward and out of the hole cut through a thatched roof. Low stools once again surrounded the fire as if it was a place where people regularly sat and talked the evening away.

Steve's attention returned to the old Völva, who was standing looking in his direction and observing him with an intent look of interest. It was a look that sent a shiver up Steve's spine. As if her gaze looked deep within him and observed the soul at the centre of his being. Eventually she indicated for Steve to take a seat by the fire. Not wanting to be in the same predicament that he found himself in with Inga, Steve selected the seat at the side of the fire closest to the door from which he had entered the building. He did not want his exit cut off by the Völva. The Völva smiled at this obvious choice and sat down on a stool of her own, adjacent to Steve.

"How did you know my name?" asked Steve.

"What do you mean?" replied the Völva.

"You called me to come in by my name. You can't possibly know my name."

"But I do." replied the Völva. "I saw your coming in a vision many moons ago. It was foretold that you would arrive to help a soul in their final moment of need. It would be you that would release them from their earthly shackles."

"What do you mean by that? And which spirit?" Steve asked.

The old Völva paused a moment and shrugged. Before speaking she picked up two wooden goblets from the side of her stool, into which she ladled the simmering red liquid from the caldron. She passed one to Steve who hesitated before taking a drink.

"Don't worry." said the Völva, "It's just a herb infused wine. It will help fortify you ready for the tasks you need to complete."

Steve still hesitated, but when he saw the Völva take a drink, he did likewise and was pleasantly surprised. It tasted very similar to the home made mulled wine that his mother prepared at Christmas. Last Christmas being the first time he had officially been allowed to try it, but this drink had a slightly more fragrant after taste.

"You didn't answer my question." Steve stated.

"You're quite right. I didn't" replied the Völva. "At first I was not sure which spirit the vision referred to. This was hidden from me. But now with all that has happened in the last few days, I can say for certain that it is the spirit of Thorunn. Would you not agree?"

Steve nodded. "But what am I supposed to do?"

"That was not revealed by my visions; they only implied that you would come and that you would know what to do. One thing that did puzzle me though was the dream indicated that you would come from both close by and at the same far off. How can this be?"

Not wanting to answer without thinking, Steve

emptied the last of the contents of his wooden goblet. He didn't recall drinking it but it was now empty.

"So who killed Thorunn?" Steve finally asked.

The Völva raised an eyebrow at Steve's evasion of her question, but answered his all the same. "That is also hidden from me. No matter how hard I try to see, it is hidden in a veil of clouds that I cannot see through."

"Why can't you see through?" Steve asked. "You saw that I was coming long before I arrived."

"I am old and my time here grows short. I am no longer as strong as I once was."

The argument between Inga and the old Völva came back to Steve. "What were you and Inga arguing about?"

"You were stood at the window I left open for you. I believe that you heard all that is important. To tell anymore would not add to your knowledge and may only serve to cloud your judgment."

Steve looked down at his feet while he thought on what else to ask and he suddenly started upright as he dropped his goblet on the floor. His head was groggy, his vision was fuzzy and the old Völva had gone. He looked round the room and she was nowhere to be seen. More Witchcraft from the Völva thought Steve. As that was how he now considered her, a witch in every sense of the word. Then Steve noticed that there was very little heat coming from the fire and it had burned down to the point that it was now almost out. He had been asleep. He had been unconscious. The Völva had drugged him in some way, probably the mulled wine, and she had left while he slept.

Chapter Twenty Seven

Steve rose from where he had been sitting and made his way to the door with the express intention in taking in some fresh air to help clear the fuzzy after effects of the drugging. On opening the door Steve was surprised to find that it was now night and dark outside. The moon was already high in the night sky. He was not sure how long he had been unconscious but it had to have been at least two to three hours for the darkness to be complete, even if it was the depth of winter.

The groggy feeling left Steve almost as soon as he took his first breath of the fresh cool night air. All of a sudden he felt revitalised and his senses seemed to be heightened in the cold of winter. The air was crisp and fresh but at the same time tinged with the arid taste of smoke from the many village fires and as Steve looked out his eyes quickly adjusted to the darkness of the night. The snow had died down to a light flurry and the night sky was now almost clear and Steve stepped out into the depth of the night. The old Völva watched him leave from where she sat on one of the low benches at the side of the room. She was covered in furs and wore an almost quizzical look of interest on her face.

Although it had almost stopped snowing it was still windy and bitter cold and as Steve emerged an icy gust of wind whipped open his cloak, exposing him to the cold. Steve stopped and grasped the edges of the flapping cloak and fastened it tight around himself, hoping to keep out the worst of the night weather. It was at that very moment that Ragnar, dressed in his familiar white furs, emerged from an alleyway and strode briskly past. Steve almost tripped over his own feet when he saw the giant warrior but Ragnar just continued past and on his way. He was like a man who was on some sort of mission. He paid no notice to Steve, not even acknowledging his presence. Steve continued to watch as Ragnar strode across the village square with his axe hung across his back. He looked, thought Steve, to be as angry as he was in a hurry.

Steve looked back to the alleyway from where Ragnar emerged. It was the alleyway that led to the cellar where he had been held captive. It also led to Inga's home and that of Philippe. This was too much of a coincidence thought Steve.

Steve was faced with two choices. To follow Ragnar

and see where he was going in such a hurry or to go and see if he could find out where Ragnar had been and what had angered him. Steve decided that following people was not getting him anywhere, apart from left unconscious, locked in a cellar, or drugged, so it was that he set off in the direction from which Ragnar had emerged.

Fresh snow on the ground and the visibility afforded by the clear night sky meant it was easy for Steve to make out Ragnar's large footprints. He followed them with ease from the square and back through the alleyway. It was when Steve exited the alleyway at the other side things became more complicated. Ragnar's footprints seamed to crisscross themselves up and down the back alley. These in turn were mixed with one, maybe two, other sets of smaller footprints. Steve did his best to follow Ragnar's prints in amongst the jumble and they seemed to go back and forth from Inga's home to Philippe's. Although at both of these places there seemed to be no one at home. Steve listened at both doors and could hear nothing from within and after listening at Inga's door for a second time Steve built up the courage to knock. He knocked soft at first and then harder and with more volume. There was no answer. Looking back up the alley Steve noticed the log he had previously used was still under Philippe's window. So as he had already found some level of bravery in knocking at Inga's door, he thought he would grasp it while he could and have another look through Philippe's window. Steve quickly made his way back up the alley and climbed onto the snow covered log. This time he checked over his shoulder, a number of times, to ensure that no one was sneaking up on him. He certainly did not want to be caught unawares again.

Steve managed to peer through a crack in the windows wooden shutters but it was dark inside and he was about to give up and step down when his eyes readjusted to the gloom within. Probably due to the low level glow from the fire pit thought Steve. There was no sign of Philippe inside, or anyone else. Steve noticed though that a number of Philippe's knives were missing from their holder on the wall. Four gaps in all. Most likely being carried by the assassin himself thought Steve as he subconsciously felt for the familiar shape of his own dagger wrapped safe within his ever present backpack.

With the thought of Philippe and his knives now at the forefront of Steve's thoughts, he was sure he heard the tell-tale crunch of a footstep in the snow somewhere behind him. Steve quickly spun round on top of the log and overbalanced. He landed in a heap in the deep snow and when he looked up scrambling backwards to protect himself. There was no one anywhere to be seen.

Steve stood and dusted himself down. He seemed to be doing that a lot lately. Then he once again looked around as if expecting to see someone. But the alley was deserted.

"Where is everyone?" Steve asked out loud and to himself. Before checking again to make sure he was alone.

It was a late winter's night and Ragnar, Inga and Philippe were all out and about somewhere. Steve had no idea about Inga or Philippe but he had just seen Ragnar. There was only one course of action to take, thought Steve. To try and catch up with Ragnar.

Steve turned away from the alley and started back towards the village square. Ragnar had a good head start on Steve now but Steve had seen the direction that he had been heading. So Steve set off at a run to try and catch up with the warrior. This time though rather than the pain and clumsiness that Steve normally associated with running. He felt light and fast on his feet, in a way that he could not easily explain. All the same he was grateful for the good fortune. Steve crossed the village square and followed Ragnar's large footprints through a narrow gap between two buildings and into the gloom.

Steve's eyes once again adjusted to the gloom as he weaved his way back and forth through the various alleys and passages that wove their way through the buildings on this side of the village. All the time Steve had an uneasy feeling he was being followed. Twice since he had crossed the square Steve was sure that he had heard someone approaching from behind, but each time he stopped and checked, there was no one to be seen. All the same Steve continued on with care, straining at the limits of his hearing as he continued with his search for Ragnar.

A third time, Steve thought he once again heard footsteps approaching, only for there to be no sign of anyone. But this time as he quickly rounded a corner before fully turning to face the direction he was heading, he ran straight into Ragnar. Ragnar was stood waiting, with his massive bulging arms folded across his chest. He was like a man mountain and Steve just bounced off him like he had run into a solid wall. Once again landing on his backside in the snow.

At first Steve thought his life to be forfeit and that Ragnar would certainly use his axe to separate his head from his shoulders as he sat there in the snow. Lucky for Steve it was as if Ragnar did not recognise him as the person he had chased on the night that Thorunn had been murdered. Instead of wielding his great war-axe, Ragnar reached down and gripped Steve's shoulder in his massive hand in a vice like grip. Steve flinched with pain. Then Ragnar hauled Steve to his feet and stared down at him, his brow furrows deepening as he spoke.

"What do you want boy?" Ragnar boomed. "Why are you following me?"

Steve just looked back up at Ragnar. His fear building until it tightened its vice like grip around his vocal chords, preventing him from answering.

Ragnar shook Steve roughly by the shoulder as if he was nothing more substantial than a Childs rag doll.

"Well I'm waiting." Ragnar said.

Steve had never come across anyone like Ragnar and was in such a state of fear and panic that he struggled to collate his words in any form of cohesion and blurted out the first thing that came into his head.

"I'm just following you to see where you are going. Seeing if I can follow a season warrior without being spotted." It even sounded stupid to Steve, but in the state he was in Steve forgot to translate it into the Viking dialect. Ragnar's grip tightened further on Steve's shoulder causing him to sag at his knees.

"Fool. Simpleton." Ragnar said as he easily threw Steve to one side, unceremoniously and face first into the snow. "Be gone with you. I have no time for the village idiot this night."

Ragnar turned and continued on his way leaving Steve, after the force of the impact, struggling to get back to his feet. Steve dusted the snow off himself once again. Then he checked himself over and was surprised to discover himself intact and without injury apart from an aching shoulder blade.

On standing, Steve looked towards the direction Ragnar had set off, not sure what to do next. Although it was probably dangerous to do so, as he didn't want to anger Ragnar anymore, Steve decided that he had no choice but to continue on his current course of action. He set off after Ragnar.

Just as Steve was about to head off after Ragnar, he felt that familiar sensation of a static build up. Steve shook his head. This was the last thing he wanted. He didn't want to Time-Walk. He didn't want to go back to present day. He felt he was so close to finding out what was going on. Steve braced himself and focused on the Viking village. He pushed away at any concept of his own place in time and tried to cling to his current reality. It worked. A moment later the static charge dissipated and Steve was still where he wanted to be.

Steve's battle with the pull of time along with the fact that Ragnar's size meant he had a huge stride and even at a jog, Steve was struggling to catch up with him. Steve was just starting to think that he had lost him again when he heard someone call out from ahead in the darkness. Then the call was followed by a muffled thump.

Steve slowed down not wanting to run into Ragnar again. Or anyone else that may be out and about.

At first Steve could see nothing, even though his eyesight had adjusted remarkably well to the gloomy darkness of the back alleyways. He continued cautiously making his way forward while listening for any further sounds. But he heard nothing. Then Steve almost tripped over something in the darkness. Steadying himself at the last moment, he looked down. There at his feet was the still and silent figure of Ragnar. His furs were almost hiding him in the white snow. Steve stepped back expecting Ragnar to stand and once again vent his anger. But Ragnar just lay there. Face down in the snow.

It was then that Steve noticed the deep red blood, slowly spreading into the whiteness of fur and snow. There at its centre and in between Ragnar's broad shoulder blades was the glint of a dagger. One of Philippe's daggers.

Chapter Twenty Eight

ot wanting to dwell overly long on the fallen and motionless body of Ragnar, Steve looked away. It became obvious to him when he had found the dying Thorunn that he did not have the stomach for real life blood, guts and gore. Instead he kept his head raised and focused on a point ahead. Off in the distance and darkness, between the buildings that lined the narrow alleyway. He took the time to recompose himself. Finding the huge warrior face down in the snow had been not only unforeseen, but a shock to his system and he needed the time to calm himself and slow his rapid beating heart. This took some doing under the circumstances. Eventually, Steve was once again calm.

Just as the Calmness had come to Steve, it fled just as quick. Steve once again heard the soft crunch of slightly frozen snow, being compressed under someone's foot. Steve stood motionless and strained his hearing to listen for what was out there in the darkness. Almost expecting as before there to be nothing but the silence of the winter's night. This time though it was not to be. As Steve listened, he heard it again. It was a definite footfall in the snow. This time a heavy scraping accompanied the footsteps. It was as if something large and metallic rang out as it caught on something. Probably Ragnar's missing war-axe, thought Steve. Whoever was out there was doing their best to move quiet as to avoid detection but Steve had heard them and now he was sure he was not alone. Whoever had killed Ragnar was still out there.

Now Steve was sure that someone was definitely out there. He was more than sure that they were approaching, following him What Steve could not be sure of was from which direction they were approaching. Or who it was.

Steve's sense of terror once again began to rise and his heart beat was now strong and fast, pounding within his chest. He was close to being frozen to the spot in terror when common sense finally prevailed. Steve did not want to be discovered here, even if the person he had heard was not his stalker. He did not want to be found standing over the fallen warrior's body and to be blamed for what had happened. After all he was still carrying a dagger identical to the one protruding from between Ragnar's shoulder blades. This, along with the reason he was out in such bad weather following the warrior, was not something that Steve wanted to try and explain away. Also on the flip side thought Steve, was that if it was Ragnar's killer that approached, Steve did not want to be on the sharp end of one of Philippe's daggers or Ragnar's axe.

Steve took what was in reality nothing more than a best guess and headed off in the direction in which he had been following Ragnar. He hoped that whoever had felled the giant was not now in front of him. Steve gradually picked up his pace until he was almost running. All of the time he was aware that he may have made a mistake and be running straight into fatal danger and ultimately the possible jaws of death.

The view forward was largely obscured by the continual curve of the narrow lane that Steve now found himself in and the fear was growing in him that his choice had been wrong and he was, in fact, running into a rather unpleasant trap. Steve slowed until he was walking and then he stopped. He stood and listened.

Even though Steve could now somehow see remarkably well in the dark, the buildings acted as a barrier to the range of his vision. Steve could see nothing or no one, either following him or in front. But at the same time his heightened senses seemed to be screaming at him. He was in danger and that danger was drawing closer. Remaining still, Steve once again listened for the giveaway crunch of snow underfoot. All Steve wanted to do was run as fast as he could, to get away from there, but he held his nerve and stayed still. It was not long before his patience was rewarded as the sound of footsteps was still there. This time slightly further away. In running Steve had opened a gap on his hunter which meant they were definitely behind him. They were tracking like he was a hunter's prey.

After a moment the footsteps stopped. Whoever was out there was for now looking to keep their distance and remain hidden from Steve. They were, thought Steve, now most likely stood like him, listening for their adversary to make the next move in this hunt.

Philippe sprang to mind instantly and unaided. He was out and about with at least one more dagger still in his possession. Two if he had stopped to retrieve the one from between Ragnar's shoulder blades. Then the thought of Ragnar's great war-axe sprang to mind. It was no longer with Ragnar and he had heard the metallic scraping that said whoever was following him now had the weapon. It had to be Philippe. He was an assassin and probably one of the few capable of getting the better of, and killing the formidable warrior. Philippe was a born killer.

This realization on top of the terror of being hunted almost caused Steve's knees to buckle from under him. What was he to do? How could he ever hope to win out against a seasoned killer like Philippe? Steve was now regretting resisting the walk back to the safety of his own 'here and now'. It may have been the biggest and last mistake of his life. It just wasn't fair.

Steve stood statue still and quiet, not wanting to give his hunter any more of an advantage, as he considered his options. He thought about his parents. Of his father's precise and methodical way of doing anything and everything. He thought of his mother's temper. But most of all he thought of how if he failed and died here in the Viking village, he would never see them again. Also how much it would hurt them; not knowing what had happened to their son in the same way as Tyler's family had in the past. It would be like history repeating itself. With these thoughts at the forefront of his mind the considerations did not take long, as no matter what he thought of it always came back to the same thing. Run and run for his life.

Steve once again heard the footsteps. His hunter was no longer still and they were most likely moving in for the kill thought Steve. The panic was building but with the thoughts of his parents still so vivid in his mind, Steve took one footstep. Then he took another and another until he was once again running through the villages winding lanes.

Steve's aim was to open a gap between him and his hunter and get somewhere relatively safe. This would give him time to think. He needed to come up with some sort of plan. Finally emerging from the twisting jumble of lanes and buildings at the large wall that surrounded the village, Steve had a distinct feeling of deja-vu. He had been chased through the village once before. That time by Ragnar, and he had landed flat on his face under the falling sweep of the axe. Steve did not want to repeat that mistake, as he doubted that he would not be so lucky a second time. So once again Steve slowed to nothing more than a brisk walk as he started to traverse the boundary wall, maintaining a pace that was safe, but not slow.

As he progressed Steve noticed for the first time on any of his visits to this Viking period that the biting cold wind had dropped and the snow had stopped. Then no, it had not dropped but had changed direction. It had lost its icy chill and was now blowing in from the south and with it came the first drops of rain. In the distance a low, faint but distinctive rumble of thunder could be heard.

Pulling his cloak close around him, so to keep dry, Steve pressed on. He was always conscious of the menacing presence of someone following and stalking him, but now the presence was only at the edge of Steve's heightened senses. Steve took this to mean that he had been successful in opening a gap on his hunter. Probably thought Steve, down to the weight of the axe slowing them down, which was designed for a much bigger man.

Steve continued working his way round the perimeter wall until he was back in familiar territory and he turned into the alley that led up to where Inga, Philippe and the old Völva all lived. He was not sure why, apart from it being his best bet for safety that he made his way to Inga's door. After all she had been the one who saved him when he had been thrown unconscious into the cellar.

On reaching Inga's door, Steve knocked before he had fully stopped. This resulted in a sound that was more of a loud bang than a knock, as if in desperation. There was no answer. Steve looked round to check he was still alone before once again knocking. This time as he knocked he lifted the latch and opened the door.

"Inga?" Steve called.

It was dark inside and Steve could see no sign of movement. The fear of what was behind him spurred Steve on and he stepped into the darkness.

"Hello?" Steve called again. "Inga?"

There was nothing in response only the silence and a clap of thunder outside. This time it was closure, causing Steve to jump and slam the door closed behind him.

At first the darkness was complete and almost stifling, but Steve's eyes soon adjusted. The darkness brightened into a gloom that allowed Steve to make out shapes within the room. Ashes within the central fire pit were long cold indicating that it had been some time since Inga had been there. Steve was not exactly happy about being alone in the dark, but at least he was indoors and out of sight from whoever was stalking him.

Hopefully Philippe would not find him here.

Steve settled into the darkness. Even if he dared, he did not have any way of lighting any of the torches that hung to the walls. The fire was out and he did not own matches or a lighter. So he resigned himself to wait in the dark hoping that Inga would return soon.

After a short period of pacing round and making several circuits of the small confines of Inga's home, Steve decided that this was doing him no good. It only served in heightening his growing feeling of fear and inevitability. A quick look around the room confirmed that there were only three options for Steve to sit, the floor, one of the crude stools around the now cold fire pit or the bed with its furs and skins. The first two did not appeal so Steve settled for the latter and dropped onto the bed next to a pile of animal skins in an attempt to keep warm.

Steve had been sitting waiting for around fifteen minutes he estimated and Still Inga had not returned. Inactivity caused his mind to race. What if Philippe had also done for Inga? Where would he turn for help? Could he just go to another of the Vikings and hope for the best? Rain could now be clearly heard outside. The continuing peals of thunder were now much closer and accompanied by flashes of lightening. The ozone filled air only heightening Steve's continually growing feeling of dread.

The damp had worked its way through Steve's cloak and he now started to feel cold, on top of everything else. Steve slid back on the bed until his back was against the wall and pulled his knees close to his chest. He hugged them in an attempt to keep warm. Although this worked in warming him initially, its relief was short lived, so Steve reached for one of the animal skins to aid with the warming. After all thought Steve, Inga would probably not mind. The first skin was only small, so Steve reached over to grab another. Instead his hand closed around something else, something that felt cold, damp and sticky to the touch. Not wanting to, but not being able to stop himself, Steve looked down just as the lightening once again illuminated the room. There from beneath the pile of skins and furs, was a blood soaked human hand.

"No!" cried Steve as he jumped from the bed.

Chapter Twenty Nine

Protruding from beneath the pile of furs and skins, giving it the look of an almost disembodied apparition, the hand now hung off the side of the bed, flaccid and unmoving. It was almost unreal in appearance in the low muted light of the depths of the night. The skin looked to be grey with black stains, arranged into some arcane symbology, streaked across its surface. It was only during the occasional flash of lightning, that the pale tones of dead skin, soaked in a dark crimson of dried blood were shown for the gruesome sight they truly were.

It was yet another body. This time here in Inga's home. It looked as if someone had made a crude attempt to hide it. As if wanting to delay the discovery. Maybe until they had time to dispose of it later. Surely later was now. What better time to dispose of a body unseen than the dead of the night during a storm? Or, thought Steve, the body was probably hidden to give the killer time to do what they needed to do and clear up any loose ends, before making a run for it. It suddenly occurred to Steve that he could well be one of those loose ends. That was why he was been followed.

Sudden flash and then a thunder clap, almost overhead now, caused Steve to jump, as if someone had sneaked up on him and tapped him on the shoulder. Steve scanned the room, more as a result of his heightened level of nervousness than anything else, but he was still alone, except for the body on the bed.

Then a panic of a thought made its way from Steve's subconscious to the forefront of his mind. This was Inga's house and Inga's bed so the body may well be that of Inga. Then the panic of the thought rose further in Steve. If this was Inga, then who was going to help him. Steve was here, trapped, out of his own time. By the look of everything that was happening, he was running out of time in every sense of the word.

"Inga?" Steve asked, more out of desperation than hope, but all remained silent.

Steve stood not moving but staring at the hand. He was trying to build up the courage to step forward and remove the animal skins to get a closer look. He needed to know for sure who the body was, whether it was Inga or not. The problem was that his stomach churned slightly at the thought. This along with the building panic caused Steve to further put off what needed to be done. He was only fourteen. This was his third body. Fourth if you count the fact that he had witnessed Thorunn die twice. No one his age should have to cope with this much gore and death. It just wasn't fair.

Steve looked away from the bed and the hand, down to his feet and realised that he was frantically rubbing his hands together. He pulled them apart dropping them to his sides and tried to force himself to relax. Taking deep, slow breaths and concentrating on the sound of his own rapid heartbeat, Steve tried to pull himself together. After a moment he felt slightly calmer and his heart had slowed. The panic was still there but Steve had managed to push it to one side and through a force of will, was holding it in check.

Returning his focus back to the hand and therefore the body that would be connected to it, Steve felt his panic start to rise once more, but after a short inner battle, he managed to hold onto the level of calmness that he had achieved. Steve stepped forward and reached out for the skins that covered the body. At first he pulled his hand away, instinct taking hold of his motor function. Then he reached out and slowly removed one of the animal skins. Then another. Until eventually the body was all but uncovered. In the dim light of the room, even with his heightened level of night vision, Steve could not make out who it was that lay before him. Whoever lay here was slight of build but the body was twisted. They were at an odd angle and face down, partially hidden by their winter cloak. Steve realised he was going to have to reach deep inside for even more courage and take hold of the body and turn it over.

Taking a large gulp of air, Steve pushed back the bile that was now rising from his guts and took hold of the still figure by the shoulder and the hip and pulled. With a heave the body turned and due to its light weight faster than Steve expected. Just as it finished turning a flash of lightning momentarily illuminated the room. The face of the assassin, Philippe, contorted into an agonising death mask, looked vacantly up at Steve.

Taking a step backward and stumbling over his own feet, Steve ended up sitting, hard, onto the dirt floor. Comprehending what he had just seen, Steve's mind reeled. He had been sure that Philippe was the killer. He was the assassin. He was probably the only person that could quickly dispatch Ragnar. It had been Philippe that had been shunned by Thorunn when she had accepted her apparent vocation in life; to be the next Völva. But he was wrong. Here lay Philippe and he was quite definitely dead.

Steve hauled himself back to his feet and once again stepped closer in order to get a better look at Philippe's body. There were no sign of a dagger, or even a stab wound like the other victims. Instead the side of

215

Philippe's head was covered in clotted blood. It had run down the side of his face and onto his clothing before drying in place. It was not the type of wound that came from a bladed weapon such as a dagger, or even an axe. Instead it looked like a viscous clubbed blow had caught him on the temple and caved in the whole side of his skull, forever contorting Philippe's once sharp features.

As Steve examined the body, his foot caught on something protruding from beneath the bed, sending it rolling back into the shadows. Kneeling down Steve reached into the darkness feeling around for what he had kicked and almost immediately found what he was looking for. It was long and wooden, almost like the thick end of a pool cue. Steve pulled it from under the bed and took it to the window, where he would have slightly more light, in which to examine it. It was an ornately hand carved staff, in some sort of dark hardwood. It was very similar to the one that Steve had seen Thorunn and the Völva carry. At its top Steve noticed mattered hair stuck to the wood with what Steve surmised to be dried blood. Steve had found the weapon which had killed the assassin.

The staff was not topped with a metallic jewelled cap. So therefore was not the old Völva's and Thorunn's had been buried with her. So unless someone had been digging in her grave, it could not be hers. The only explanation left was that it belonged to Inga. This made

216

sense as this was Inga's home and if Inga followed the same path as her sister, then she too would have her own staff or wand. Philippe had been killed with Inga's staff.

With another flash of light and crack of thunder, realisation dawned. Steve realised how stupid he had truly been. He had become so convinced as time had progressed that Philippe the assassin was back living up to his name and profession, that he had not considered that there may be alternatives. That it was someone else responsible for Thorunn's murder. Now here it was. Staring him full in the face. Inga was the killer.

The reason Inga had been able to rescue him from the food cellar was not because she had been in the right place at the right time to observe someone dump his unconscious body down there. No. It was due to the fact that it had been Inga herself that had crept up on him. She knocked him out and dumped him into the dark cellar. Only to return later and play the heroin. That was if that had been her plan. Maybe she had come back to see if he was dead, or even finish off the job. Steve shuddered at the thought.

Then to add insult to injury she had befriended and chatted with him while giving him shelter. Probably just to find out what he was up to, what he knew and suspected. Then using the information to stay one step ahead of him all the time.

By now Steve had made his way back to the bed,

where he sat down. Almost flopping onto the bed. The strength seeming to leave him, but at the same time making sure he kept at least some distance between himself and Philippe's corpse.

Steve did not know what he was going to do or what he could achieve. Inga was supposed to be his ally here in the Viking village, but instead she was the enemy within. She had been systematically taking care of anyone that may get in her way. So now he was alone, facing a bleak future in the past and with no one to turn to. What could he do?

Just then, as Steve was slipping into the depths of self-sorrow and depression, the door flew open with such force that it clattered off the wall behind it, almost rebounding closed before slowly swinging wide open once more. At first Steve had thought it was the wind that had blown it open. As it had once again picked up during the thunder storm that raged all around.

Steve was just standing to go and close the door when a long sustained flash of lightning illuminated a solitary figure in the door way. The wind had not burst open the door. It was Inga. She was standing there with manic rage on her face and Ragnar's huge double bladed war-axe in her hands. Inga had come for Steve.

Chapter Thirty

ightning flashed across the sky once more, jagged and vicious, providing a high angled illumination of Inga's face. The contrast of shadows and highlights giving it the appearance of a grotesquely twisted Halloween mask, anger and madness etched deeply into every feature. Gone was the friendly facade that Inga had previously presented to Steve on their night talking in comfort around her cooking fire. Replaced with what Steve now surmised was what had been all along, the true face of the murderess.

Steve looked round the room, his head frantically snapping back and forth as he searched for an alternative exit. He needed a way to get away from Inga and more important a way to escape with his life. But this was to no avail as the only way out was through the main door and that was currently blocked by Inga.

The moment was broken by a loud thud echoing around the room as Inga dropped the double bladed end of Ragnar's great war-axe onto the ground. She lent upon it in a pose of mocked composure, with her hands folded, on its leather bound handle. Only the white knuckles of her tightly clenched fingers portrayed a different story. Rather than serene composure it was one of fear, anger and madness boiling within.

Inga stood framed in the doorway, seemingly much larger and more imposing than the physicality of her slight feminine frame. She stared. Not moving. Not even speaking at first, with the appearance of someone who had not slept for several days. Her red framed, bloodshot eyes fixed on Steve, then narrowed.

"Well?" she finally said.

"What do you mean?" replied Steve.

"Well! What I mean is I am going to have to kill you now. It's all your fault. I didn't want to do it. I even liked you. You're a nice boy. But I have to do it. As I said it's entirely your fault."

Inga took a first step forward, entering the threshold of her home. The axe scraping on the floor as she moved, the tone of the metal on the hard packed earth floor producing a dull ringing that seemingly announcing to Steve his impending doom.

"No wait!" Steve said, stopping Inga in her tracks. "Why is it all my fault? Why do I have to die?

Inga looked at Steve as if it should be obvious, like he was some sort of village simpleton. Then, after a moment's pause, she gave a smile that touched nothing but her lips and she started to explain anyway.

"It's quite simple. Like all the others you've come too close." Inga said.

"Others? You mean Ragnar and Philippe?" Steve asked glancing briefly at the French assassin's motionless corpse, before quickly returning his full attention to Inga.

"Who else would I mean?" asked Inga as she took another step further into the room and closer to Steve. He in turn searched and racked his brain for a way to continue to stall Inga. He needed to give himself time to try and come up with a way to get away from her.

"What do you mean by too close?" he finally asked. It was all he could think of under pressure.

"Starting with Ragnar, our so called beloved protector!" Inga said, spitting to the ground, in contempt, as she spoke, only just stifling the start of a manic laugh. "To start with he was sure it was an outsider that killed Thorunn. You in fact. After all he had seen you leaning over her still warm body."

"But, what changed his mind?" Asked Steve, hoping to keep Inga distracted with her telling.

"I've already told you that Ragnar had a bit of a temper. But after he got over his original rage and the confusion of you eluding him in the chase. And that; I wish we had time for you to tell me how you managed it. But as I was saying, he calmed down and realised that you were just a boy. Not yet a man and no match for Thorunn. You would never have even got close enough to her to do any harm. She would have sensed it within you."

"But how did he get too close to you?" Steve pressed.

"Don't interrupt me boy, or I'll end your miserable, interfering existence here and now!"

Steve made an exaggerated show of shutting his mouth. Partially to show compliance, but mainly due to not wanting to infuriate Inga further who was now becoming more manic as she spoke, rushing what she was saying and hardly pausing for breath.

"As I was saying." Inga Continued. "Ragnar quickly discounted the possibility that it could be a stranger like you. And that train of thought quickly had him realising that it had to be someone close to Thorunn. Someone who could get close to her without suspicion. He was as equally quick to discount the possibility that it could have been Philippe. As even though Philippe was on the angry side of upset at loosing Thorunn, he still loved her too much to do her any harm. So that and the fact that he discovered Philippe's body here left him with only one conclusion..."

"Ragnar found Philippe's body?" asked Steve.

"Yes. He wasn't supposed to but he did and then he stormed out of here after me. But I was watching from a rooftop and he a mere man could never hope of catching me. Thorunn was not the only one in our family strong with the ways of the Völva."

"So you followed him and killed him?" asked Steve as Inga took another step forward.

"Followed him yes. Kill him no. Well not at first. I was going to but then I spotted you in your feeble attempt at following the oaf. That opened a whole new opportunity and I wanted to give you enough rope to hang yourself."

"And how was I supposed to do that?" asked Steve.

"Simple, if I noticed you following Ragnar, then there would be a high chance that others would have as well. Once his body is discovered, you'd be blamed, the outsider assassin, the stranger in our midst. And I intend to encourage this belief. Then just after he chased you off, he turned to see if you were still following and I stepped out behind him. I brought the blade down and drove it home. It was so simple to bring down the supposed champion warrior. No problem at all." Inga answered.

"But Philippe. Why kill Philippe? Was he also onto you?" asked Steve now desperate to keep the conversation going and prolong his life.

Inga continued. "Yes. He had also worked it out, but almost from the off and much faster than the oaf of a warrior. After all he had suspected how I truly felt about my sister, even though she had been blind to it. He was dangerous and too intelligent for his own good. He had

223

loved Thorunn unconditionally and would have never have rested until he had proven me the killer. He didn't just want revenge, he wanted justice and to destroy the life of power I have planned for myself. There was no questioning it; Philippe simply had to die."

Inga stepped yet closer to Steve and he now found himself with his back firmly against the wall, He had not realised he had moved from where he had been standing when Inga burst open the door, but he had, and now he was left with nowhere to go.

"He made the big mistake of turning his back on me when he came here to confront me earlier this evening. You would be surprised at how well I can swing my staff." Inga continued.

Desperate for Inga not to finish talking for he knew that the end of her tale would signal the end of his life, Steve continued his line of questioning. "But how do you expect to get away with it all. With all these killings someone will work it out, the old Völva will be bound to realise that there was a pattern. That it was you."

Inga sneered at Steve's presumptions then continued. "There will be nothing to work out. After all, the village will have their killer. They will have you, or more accurately they will have their killer's body."

Steve swallowed, trying in vain to bring moisture to his now dry mouth, dry through the thought of his impending demise a millennium before his own time. He was alone and away from the parents he loved. It just wasn't fair.

"But why should they believe you?" asked Steve, "And what about the Völva?"

"The daggers, you stupid boy, the daggers." Inga answered.

"What about the daggers?" Steve asked.

"Don't think I didn't see you stuff that dagger into your pack that night in the cellar. I don't know how you came by it but it was defiantly one of Philippe's."

Steve just looked at Inga, not comprehending what she was saying.

"It's the same as the ones used to kill Thorunn and Ragnar and the same as this one." Inga indicated a matching assassin's dagger neatly tucked into her rope belt. "This is the one which I'll use to dispatch the old crone of a Völva, just as soon as I've finished dealing with you."

At this, Steve's face drained to that of ashen white, as realisation hit him and Inga's face once more twisted into the smile of a mad woman.

"And then, when they search my body, they'll find mine. Thus incriminating me as the killer." Steve stated.

"Yes exactly. You the stranger assassin in our midst."

A faint shuffling sound caught Steve's attention. It was almost inaudible, at the very edge of his enhanced range of hearing, but then, almost immediately, it was gone and once more. It was silent. Steve berated himself, had his chance to alert someone of what was going on slipped him by? Had he missed his chance to escape? In desperation he yelled out at the top of his voice. He was now hoarse due to the dryness of his mouth and throat, causing him to produce an inaudible scream rather than coherent words. But Steve was now fighting for his life and he screamed until his voice finally faltered.

Sometime before Steve had finished crying out for help Inga had thrown her head back in a crazy rolling peal of laughter. It was laughter that sent a chill of realisation through Steve, realisation that there was going to be no escape for him this time. He fought his emotions and struggled to hold back the tears, and at least maintain some form of dignity.

Steve did not hear the end of Inga's laugh, but it must have ended because she was now once again silent and looking at him with an unblinking stare.

"There's no one about to help you. No one will be out and about in a storm like this. No one to hear you. Just you, me and this axe." Inga stated.

Thunder overhead, the loudest yet accompanied with sheet lightning, illuminating the underside of the continually building storm clouds, seemed to emphasise what Inga had just said. Steve let his shoulders sag.

"Are you not going to beg for me to spare your miserable life?" asked Inga.

Steve slowly shook his head back and forth as he looked down at his own feet, taking a few seconds to quietly gather himself. Then he ran, charging at Inga. With a sudden burst of speed. It was a last ditch attempt for freedom and for his life. Briefly his spirits were lifted slightly as Inga stepped to one side, as if to avoid his impact and let him past. Steve could clearly see through the doorway and into the open and he increased his effort to get there. Inga's side step had just been a calculated feint and she casually stuck her foot out into Steve's path.

Steve's momentum meant that he could not avoid the trip. The attempt to do so just served to send him sprawling at an angle and into the wall to the side of the door. Steve hit the wall then the ground hard, knocking the wind out of him and leaving him a little dazed.

When he looked up, Steve's shoulder cried out in pain and his way to the door was once again blocked by Inga, but now his situation had visibly deteriorated, as Inga was looming over him. Her face once again a calculated mask of calm and the axe now held, ready to drop, and finish Steve off once and for all.

Chapter Thirty One

Steve scrambled across the floor trying his best to back away from Inga and the axe. This proved difficult due to the fact that he was already up against the wall and his right shoulder cried out in pain each time he put any weight on it. The only direction open to Steve was towards the corner of the room. This was far from ideal as it took him away from the only door and any chance of freedom.

A wicked grin crossed Inga's face as she watched Steve wince in pain. She raised and swung the axe bringing it to bear with much more agility and speed that Steve had thought possible. The blade almost whistled as it arched through the air and rushed towards him. Equally as quick Steve's reflexes over rode the pain he was feeling and he abandoned scrambling and instead just rolled away from Inga. As he did the axe blade buried itself into the hard packed dirt floor, where only a second earlier he had been lying.

Inga tugged furiously at the axe, trying to free if from where it had buried itself in the floor. She worked the handle so that it rocked back and forth so to free it and continue her deadly attack.

Steve knew his life was over if he didn't stall her. He needed the time to manoeuvre himself into a position that he could try and use to his advantage.

"So you just killed your own sister?" asked Steve.

Inga didn't reply and continued working the axe.

"What about Thorunn?" Steve pressed.

That seemed to flip a switch in Inga's mind and she stopped struggling with the axe. "What about Thorunn? It was all about Thorunn. It always was!"

"So you hated her so much you killed her?" continued Steve.

"Yes I hated her that much." Inga replied. "She had the life that should have been mine."

This time Steve remained silent, waiting for Inga to elaborate. All the time his heart pounded like a drum in his ears as he sought an opportunity to act.

"She was the older you see." Inga continued. "Just by a few minutes. But still the older. The first born."

"But what difference does that make?" Steve asked.

"All the difference in the world. Even as children she was always introduced first. We were always 'Thorunn and her sister', never the other way round. It just wasn't fair!"

Inga returned her attention to trying to free the axe, which finally came free.

"So you killed her just because of that?" Steve asked, trying to keep the conversation going.

"Not just that, but that and everything it stood for. Right up to her being named as successor to the Völva. It wasn't fair. I was stronger. It should have been me. I even tried to convince that old crone, but no. It had to be Thorunn, the elder. It was this that supposedly equipped her with the temperament that was necessary. What does she know?" Inga said, almost frothing at her mouth, with the effort of getting it off her chest.

"So that's what the old Völva meant when she said that she would not allow it?" Steve asked.

This statement only served to push Inga over the top. Her face now red with rage. "You heard that!" Inga lifted the axe from where it was resting since she had freed it. She hefted it ready to swing and once again Steve tried to move out of the reach of its blade.

"You are only putting off the inevitable." Taunted Inga, as she closed in on Steve leaving him nowhere to go.

As a last ditch attempt at distracting Inga, Steve pulled off his back pack and threw it at her causing her to pause. But only for a moment as she easily side stepped the projectile. The moment was enough for Steve to move to one side away from Inga and towards the bed, which he used to pull himself to his feet.

"Ha!" Inga spat. "You can't get away. I'm going to kill you. Then the old crone. Then the future will be mine. Then life will be fair!" Inga said.

"Life isn't fair." Steve blurted. "It's life, it is what it is, what you make of it. But it doesn't owe it to you to be fair."

At this Inga exploded in rage and started to swing the axe wildly in huge arcs, and Steve just managed to avoid the first two swings. As Inga recovered from the latest of her swings, Steve decided that it was his last chance and made another dash. This time not for the door and outside, but instead directly at Inga.

As Steve looked Inga in the eye he knew he had made a mistake, but he was already committed. A glint in her eye revealed that she had read him and showed the joy at his foolish childish attempt. It was just then that Inga brought up her foot, which made contact with Steve's groin. The combined force of Steve's momentum and Inga's kick dropped Steve to floor where he rolled into a ball in agony.

Inga howled with manic laughter at Steve's evident pain and her moment of triumph as she stood over his still riving form. She raised the axe ready to deliver the killer blow as once again lightning flashed as if to emphasise the end of Steve's life. All Steve could see, as he looked up, was the razor sharp blade as it rose above him. Everything else faded into insignificance as the moment of his own mortal demise stretched out in front of him. The blade completed it upwards arc, paused a minute moment of time then started its downward arc, gathering speed as it was swung. Out of options Steve could almost hear the call of death as he pulled his legs up to his chest and curled tightly into a ball, resigned to his fate.

Then there was nothing. Just silence. It took Steve a moment to realise that he was not dead.

A huge hand was wrapped around the handle of the axe, holding it in place where it had been stopped in mid stroke. Steve had been saved and saved by Ragnar.

Inga let out a scream. It was one mixed with rage and disappointment at been thwarted as she turned from Steve and faced the warrior. Who Steve now realised was leaning on the old Völva for support.

With a scream of "It's not fair!" Inga released her grip on the axes handle and let it tumble to the floor. She took a step back and pulled the dagger from her rope belt. Still screaming she lunged at Ragnar. Her hand held overhead, dagger held tightly in her fist.

Ragnar responded at once by pushing the old Völva to one side and out of Inga's reach while at the same time raising his arm to block Inga's lunge. He managed to deflect the blow but not totally as Steve noticed a trickle of blood dripping off Ragnar's fingers. Inga had further wounded the warrior.

The effort was obviously too much for Ragnar to handle without the support of the Völva and he slumped to one side and onto his knees. Inga grinned and pressed her advantage

And slashed wildly at Ragnar, who could do little more than hold up his arms to protect himself.

"Do something." The Völva cried.

It was a call that brought Steve back into himself and he leaped to help the warrior that had come to his aid. Steve grabbed the forgotten war-axe and swung it towards Inga. It was a clumsy swing. Steve was not used to the weapon and it was too heavy for him. The axe turned in Steve's hand as he started to loose his grip. At the same time Inga became aware of the danger and turned to face Steve. She screamed in anger and once again held the dagger in a raised fist.

Then all of a sudden there was silence as Steve hit Inga full in the face with the flat of the axe head. Inga crumpled to the floor, convulsed once, and then lay in a pool of blood the spread outward from her now still form.

Ragnar exhaled and slumped against the wall, as if the effort of thwarting Inga and then defending himself had cost him all his remaining strength. For the first time when Steve looked him in the face, he thought that

Ragnar looked old, old and weary.

"Don't Just sit there gawking boy." The old Völva said. "Can't you see he's badly wounded?"

At first Steve couldn't comprehend what had just happened, but finally he responded. Ignoring his own pain, he rushed over to help the old Völva shift Ragnar gently to a sitting position on the floor. She then lent him forward so she could tend to his wound in his back, which was once again bleeding freely.

"Is he going to be OK?" Steve asked.

"In time he will be. After all a warrior does not get to his age without being as strong as a farm ox." The Völva replied as she removed a poultice from Ragnar's wound. She then reapplied a fresh mix, stemming the flow of blood almost instantly. Then when that was complete she tended the lesser wounds on the warrior's arms, taking care to clean and bandage each forearm.

"Right, let me have a look at you." The Völva said to Steve.

Steve took a hesitant step forward as the old Völva checked him over. She felt for any breaks and checked his skull and eyes for any sign of a concussion. When she had finished, to her satisfaction, she declared. "You'll be OK. Just a few bruises and those will heal pretty quickly."

"What about Inga?" Steve asked.

"Oh, she is most defiantly dead." The Völva said.

"From the moment the axe hit her in the face, I felt her evil soul leave this world."

"And Thorunn's spirit?" Steve asked. "Last time we spoke you said it remained, somehow trapped."

The old Völva paused and lifted her head slightly as if sniffing the air, then replied. "Thorunn still lingers. Can you not feel her?"

Steve was about to shake his head but then he felt something, something that hung like a warm aroma in the air. It was just at the edge of his sensory perception, a feeling of great sadness and gratitude.

"How?" asked Steve.

The potion I gave you to give you the strength I said you would need this night. It contains some of what makes us Völva, some of our magic. It lets you feel, to sense beyond what is considered to be normal, both in our world and those close to it."

"But." Steve stared.

The Völva cut in. "Don't worry. It will fade with time – a little. But it is something that will always remain with you. You will get used to it and I think it may be even of use to one like yourself"

"So I did hear you outside." Steve said.

"Yes. I wanted you to know that we were coming to help. I whispered it on the wind. I was not sure you would hear me and Ragnar was slower than I expected with his injuries."

Ragnar was dozing on the floor as Steve looked down at him and he was just about to ask about the warrior, when he gave an involuntary shiver as if a cold breeze had passed straight through him.

"She's gone?" Steve asked.

"Yes. That was Thorunn leaving. She is finally at peace thanks to you."

"How? I didn't do anything." said Steve.

"But you did, you didn't give up on Thorunn. In doing so you forced Inga's hand and you have our thanks."

Steve was about to ask more questions when the air around him crackled with static. This time Steve could not resist its draw. The sun shone, and Steve stood outside the store where his parents did their weekly shop.

Chapter Thirty Two

It had been a little over a week since Steve had stood in that small room with a Viking warrior, an old witch and two recently dead bodies and he was now back working at the dig site most days. Voluntarily at that. He was working with his father, to whom Steve had been forced to tell the story; several times. Each time with occasional comments of how lucky Steve was from his father. Although Steve had not felt lucky at the time, looking back he could see what his father meant.

The dig had been considered a huge success. They had discovered two further graves near to that of Thorunn's. The first was that of another young woman almost exact in size to Thorunn, with the exception of it looked as they had been killed by their skull being shattered. The grave had been very sparse though with no grave goods unlike Thorunn's. Steve knew this to be the remains of Inga. They must have buried her next to her sister, but without all the pomp and ceremony that had accompanied the farewells to Thorunn.

The final remains were that of a small framed man. A grave that the dig team had been very excited about. Mainly due to the fact that the body had been buried with five daggers. Not only were they all identical to each other, but they also matched the one found in the first grave. In Thorunn's grave. This set the team off on all sorts of wild theories, and Steve said nothing, but he knew it to be the grave of Philippe.

There were no other graves found in that area of Ravensby Tops that were from the same period in history. No remains of a huge warrior or those of a frail old woman. So Steve did not know what had become of Ragnar and the old Völva and he resigned himself to the fact that he probably never would. As he sat under the copse of old trees enjoying the sunshine, the circle of birds now gone and the hilltop chill just a memory. The pathway to the past that was the Viking village was once again closed to this Time-Walker.

"Dad where is Mary. I mean Professor Anderson?" Steve asked.

"Who?" His father replied.

"You know. The professor. The geophysicist."

"Never heard of her. Young Eve does all the geophysics work here."

Look Out For

THE TIME WALKER'S JOURNAL : BOOK 2

FOG BOUND

When evil comes out to play.

A supernatural serial killer roams the streets of
Victorian Durham and this time there's more than
Steve's life at risk.

5968100R00144

Printed in Great Britain
by Amazon.co.uk, Ltd.,
Marston Gate.